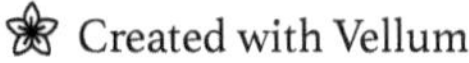 Created with Vellum

To all the good little girls

who have met a gorgeous stranger

and wondered,

"What if?"

I see you.

trigger warnings

Exhibitionism
Praise
Graphic Sexual Scenes
Edging/Orgasm Control
DD/lg Dynamics
Spitting
Cockwarming
Breeding
Gun Violence
Abduction
Pregnancy
Captivity
Narcotics
Death/Torture
Non-Consensual Sexual Touching
Threats of Sexual Assault
Human Trafficking (Mention Only)

one

ISABELLA

"You're serious?" He eyes me up and down before turning to the bartender and lifting two fingers into the air, "Two more."

"Who jokes about that?"

The bartender drops two shot glasses on the counter in front of us. He hesitates to pour the shots as he's been eavesdropping on our conversation throughout the evening.

Apparently the two of us are quite entertaining.

Eventually, he grabs the bottle and pours them full of tequila. At this point, he no longer reaches for the salt or lime, because he knows we're going to shoot them straight. We each grab one, tap it on the bar, and shoot it back.

"Never? Not even once?" He continues to pry.

"No," I adamantly shake my head at him, "Never."

"But you've..." he hesitates to finish his question as his hands gesture in the air.

"Yes, of course," I answer the question I know is looming, "I'm twenty-six..."

His finger presses against my lips before I have the opportunity to say anymore, causing my heart to flutter.

Flipping the shot glass in my hand, I place it upside down on the counter next to the others from this evening. By a quick count of the collection growing in front of us, this was my fourth in the past few hours that we've been sitting at this bar.

Liquid courage.

It's the only way to explain what is happening right now. After walking in on my boyfriend fucking my best friend and losing my job in the same week, I did what any perfectly sane, twenty-something woman with no responsibilities would do. I cried. I ate a tub of Ben & Jerry's. Or two. Then I maxed out my credit card and booked a last minute, all-inclusive trip to a resort in Mexico by myself.

Three days of margaritas, reading on the beach, and forgetting about all the shit I left behind; and now I'm sitting at the bar doing shots, spilling my deepest secrets to a man I've never met before.

A gorgeous fucking man!

While I haven't asked him many questions but his name, I am assuming he is significantly older than me by the way his hair is starting to salt-and-pepper by his temples. For a man probably old enough to be my father, he has the quite the opposite of a dad bod. Between his muscular arms, broad shoulders, rock hard pecs, chiseled abs, and that fucking V-cut leading into his board shorts, I've struggled to keep my eyes focused on his face for the hours we've been chatting. Luckily, those bright, baby-blue eyes and broad smile are also quite enticing to look at.

Yet here I am. Telling this beautiful stranger of a man my deepest sexual secrets like it's nothing.

"How many times?"

"Six," I shrug my shoulders.

"But obviously by yourself," he eyes me questioningly.

Breaking eye contact, my focus immediately goes to the ground. I can feel my cheeks raising in temperature as they turn a bright shade of red. My gaze still focused on the floor, I shake my head.

"You mean you've never made yourself come? Or you've never touched yourself?" His words sound almost shocked as though he has never heard of such a foreign concept in his life.

"Neither. I mean, no," I stammer to find the words, "No to both."

The look on his face is indistinguishable.

In an attempt to hide my embarrassment, I opt to seek some solace in the margarita sitting before me.

ALEJANDRO

After a long day of meetings, I threw on my trunks to take a quick swim in the ocean to clear my mind before heading back to New York City tomorrow morning. When that didn't work, I swung by the hotel bar to grab an Old Fashioned to take back to my villa. While waiting to order my drink, one of the most stunning women I have ever seen took the seat next to me.

She is a short little thing, can't be much more than five foot tall. Through the sheer cover-up over her bikini, it is obvious that her short stature is packed full of ample curves. Her face is classically beautiful, complete with gorgeous, pouty, pink lips. It wasn't her body or her face that enticed me to stop though. It was her curly, cherry-red hair and those emerald-green eyes that drew me in.

It's been a few hours, and I still haven't made it to my villa. I am absolutely enthralled by the woman keeping me company and have no intentions of leaving her anytime soon.

My face involuntarily scrunches in confusion as she continues to tell me how she has never had an orgasm – with a partner or by herself. She is beautiful, smart, and witty. What man wouldn't want to take the time to worship and please her?

How the fuck has she gone this long without knowing that kind of euphoric pleasure?

"Can I ask why?" I feel like I'm pushing, but this is the game we've been playing. No personal details – full names or where we live – but spill the stuff you don't tell anyone. In the short time we've been sitting here, I feel like I've learned more about her than the last five women I've dated combined.

"I guess I never really saw the point," she sips her margarita, "I've obviously had guys touch me and it didn't really do anything for me. So, I just never have."

I continue to watch her in complete bewilderment.

"And I've heard that some women can't," she shrugs as she takes another sip, "You haven't ever been with a woman, and she didn't...come?"

"Honestly? No," I reach for my glass on the bar, "The women I fuck always come, not just once, but several times."

"Oh," her eyes are big and the surprise at my words is written across her face, "maybe I'm just not like those women."

"You could be," the words slip from my mouth before I can catch them. While we have been talking for a while, that was fucking forward and presumptuous. Even for me.

But fuck, I would like her to be.

Her cheeks are no longer just pink from being sun-kissed, but now are bright red from embarrassment.

"I'm sorry, Izzy" I blurt out, "I didn't mean..."

"But didn't you?" She smirks at me and chuckles, "Be honest, Alex. No point in us having secrets from each other now."

Her head nods at the bartender and she raises two fingers at him. We sit in silence for the first time since we started talking, awkwardly waiting for him to come to our side of the bar and pour us two more shots of tequila. He has barely finished filling the first when she grabs the glass and downs it, as her cheeks begin to flush.

As I reach for my shot, she blurts out, "This is one hundred percent the tequila talking, because I would never have the courage to ask this without it..."

Watching her fidget anxiously in her seat, I throw back my shot while waiting for her to continue.

"What makes you so certain I could be like those women? That I can come?"

Turning on my stool, I spin to face her.

two

ISABELLA

I can't believe I just asked that.

I swallow hard as Alex spins on his stool to face me, while turning mine to face him. When he stops, my crossed legs are settled between his massive, muscular thighs.

Staring into my eyes, he places his large hands on my outer thighs, just above my knees. His touch immediately causes my heart to race. Never breaking eye contact, he leans in. His face slowly inching toward mine as his hands dip under my cover-up.

Is this really happening?

Or am I fucking drunk?

My heart is thumping in my chest, as his stubble dusts over my cheek and his warm breath blows over my ear, "I'm not some inexperienced college guy that is just looking for somewhere to come."

Slowly, his hands continue up my outer thighs until they are on my hips. My breasts rise and fall with every audible breath I take.

"If I had the pleasure of fucking a woman as amazing as you," his words a warm whisper against my ear, "I would want to worship every inch of you while I pleasured you."

I expect him to pull back from me, but he stays with his cheek resting against mine, his warm breath continuing to blow over my ear. My thighs squeeze together, in a futile attempt to calm this foreign, fluttering sensation at my center.

"I would play with your sweet, neglected pussy all night, not stopping until you were satisfied," his thumbs slide under the strings of my bikini bottom as his hands glide over my hips. Gripping my ass, his voice becomes deeper and gravelly, "And then I'd fuck you."

A quiet, whispery moan grumbles from my mouth as my thighs clench tightly together, fighting against a neediness I didn't know I possessed. The things this man is currently whispering into my ear are doing more to my body than the touch of any man I've ever known.

Slowly leaning back from me, his eyes meet mine. I stare back at him as his fingers delicately drag down my thighs, eliciting goosebumps in their wake, until his hands are once again by my knees.

Struggling to remember to breathe, I stare back at him in silence while my heart continues to pound in my chest. It is pounding so hard; I'm sure he must be able to hear it.

"Come," he stands from his stool and grabs my hand, pulling me from mine until I am standing next to him. Looking up at him, he is massive in comparison to me. He must be more than a foot taller than me.

"Where are we going?" I blurt out while struggling to keep up with his giant strides.

Noticing my struggle to keep up with him, he slows down his pace allowing me to walk more comfortably next to him as we reach the beach.

"Night swim," he squeezes my hand as we walk toward the rolling surf.

As the water laps at my toes, I take in how different this atmosphere is. While we aren't far from the resort's bar, it's like we walked to a different universe. The bar was loud, bright, and full of people. At this hour, the beach is deserted, quiet, and the only light is coming from the moon.

Letting go of my hand, Alex steps in front of me and leans forward until his hands are at my hips. I feel his fingers gathering my cover-up into his hands, as the thin material slowly inches up my legs until it is bunched around my waist.

"Lift," the sole word deep and commanding. Hesitantly, I lift my arms over my head. Once they are raised, he slowly glides it up my body until it clears my hands. A quiet growl rumbles from his chest as his eyes wander down this more exposed view of my body.

"You're so fucking beautiful," he reaches for my hand before pulling me into the surf.

As someone who normally doesn't go into the ocean beyond my ankles, I start to get nervous at the point the water reaches my waist. When it reaches my chest, I push onto my tippy-toes and squeeze his hand, "Alex?"

Turning around, he sees me struggling and uses his grip on my hand to pull me through the water to him. Letting go of me for a second, his large hands wrap around my waist and lift me from the water. Holding me against him with one arm, the other reaches for my hand.

"Wrap your arms around my neck," he leads my arm to his shoulders, "and your legs around my waist."

My limbs wrap around his body as he continues to lead us deeper into the water, not stopping until the water is lapping at both our shoulders and the resort looks miles away on the sand. The moonlight dances over the water around us and we bob silently with the movement of the ocean.

With one hand cupped against my ass, holding me to him, his other brushes the hair from my face and tucks it behind my ear.

"I'm going to kiss you now, *cerecita*," his fingers slide into my hair as he draws my face toward his.

His soft lips dust over mine, barely touching me. My lips part, giving him an invitation he quickly accepts. His tongue slowly presses into my mouth before he gently begins to explore my clit. In turn my tongue begins to explore his, the kiss slowly becoming more passionate and aggressive. His fingers tightly fist my hair and I whimper into his mouth as my legs squeeze around his waist, trying desperately to get closer to him.

Using his grip in my hair, he pulls our mouths apart. We are both breathless and panting and he pulls harder, granting him access to my neck. His lips and tongue leave a trail of aggressive wet kisses from my jaw to my collarbone and back up toward my ear.

"Let me be your first," his hand slides the length of my leg around his waist, gripping it at the ankle and slowly beginning to unwrap me from his body.

"Out here?" I sputter.

"I don't want to fuck you. At least not yet," the corner of his mouth turns up in a smirk, "Let me be the first to make you come, to show you what your body is capable of."

My head darts around, looking at the beach behind us.

"No one can see us out here," he reassures me as his hand rubs over the bottoms of my bikini causing me to groan while I chew at my lower lip.

"I can't promise no one will hear you scream," his fingers slide under the fabric and pull it to the side, granting him full access to me, "but they won't be able to see."

Before I can say anything else, his finger rubs around my entrance before beginning to press inside me.

"Relax, *cerecita*. Open up and let me in," his words rumble along my neck and over my chest as he places wet kisses between his words.

Closing my eyes and taking a deep breath, I feel him slide his finger fully inside me. Unlike the others who have touched me, he doesn't forcefully thrust it in and out of me. Instead, he flexes and bends it, slowly and gently rubbing it along a sensitive spot inside me. My thighs part, further opening myself to him.

"That's it," he growls as he pulls his finger nearly out of me, "Let me stretch out your pussy."

Pulling his finger nearly out of me, I feel him add another finger and stretch me as they both begin curling along my walls. My breathing is ragged and uncontrollable whimpers tremble over my lips as he increases the pressure and rhythm of his movements.

"You feel so tight wrapped around my fingers," he further increases his tempo inside of me, "I can only imagine how good you'll feel when I stretch you around my cock."

Never in my life has a man talked to me like this.

It feels like his words echo through my body, straight to where his fingers are diligently rubbing inside me.

His fingers begin working in and out of me as he continues to curl and flex them inside of me, and my hips begin flexing to meet his movements, needing more of him like I have never needed a man to fill me.

My whimpers turn into moans when he kisses along my neck while his fingers continue to work inside of me, "Is my good little girl going to come for me?"

A foreign flutter begins to grow at my center and my head tips back toward the water.

"I can't wait to see how fucking beautiful you are when you come undone," his teeth trail down my neck, "Be a good little girl and let me watch you come."

The flutter shoots through me like a jolt of electricity and I begin to scream out in pleasure. Alex's lips wrap over my mouth, swallowing my screams. His tongue takes my mouth as his fingers begin to slow, his continued touch making my body tremble uncontrollably against him.

As the tremble rattling through me begins to subside, he slowly pulls his fingers from me. Sliding his fingers under my suit, he adjusts my bikini bottom so that it is covering me, before wrapping my legs back around his waist.

three

ALEJANDRO

"Those boys don't know what they're missing," my words are deep and gravelly against her ear, "You're fucking gorgeous when you come."

Watching her come, made me so fucking hard. Wrapping her legs back around my waist only causes my cock to throb harder.

I want to take her bare.

Right here and now.

With her limbs wrapped around me once more, my hands cup the sides of her face before plunging my tongue into her mouth again. Her hips grind against me, rubbing her pussy over my cock. A feral groan expels from my lungs into her mouth.

Through our kiss, I feel her hand press between the two of us, reaching down toward my waist. Dragging her lower lip between my teeth, I pull away just as her hand slides beneath the waistband of my shorts. Her eyes widen and she lets out a small gasp as her fingers wrap around me and slowly slide along my length.

Fuck, her hand feels good.

"As great as that feels, *cerecita,*" reaching between us and gently grabbing her wrist, I pull her hand from my shorts, "I'm not nearly done with you."

With my hands firmly gripping her ass, she whimpers as my lips and teeth travel from her collarbone to her ear. "Come to my villa," the deep whisper, more a command than a question, "Let me show you how you deserve to be worshipped."

"Yes," she hesitantly murmurs as her head nods against my face.

Holding her body to mine, my lips continue to explore her neck and we make our way back to the shore. Reaching the sand, I wrap my arm tightly around her waist while I bend forward. The sudden movement causes her to let out a small gasp and squeeze her legs around my waist as I collect our things from the beach.

"It's going to awfully fucking difficult," I groan as I stand with our belongings, "to wait until we get to my villa to make you come again if you're going to do that."

"Do what?" Her voice is soft and innocent, as though she truly has no idea what it is she is doing to me.

"If you're going to squeeze your legs that tightly around my waist," my hands slide back under her ass to support her as I begin walking, "I want it to be with my cock buried inside of you."

I feel her breathing stutter and hear her swallow hard.

"Does that shock you?" My teeth lightly nip at her shoulder, "That I want you screaming with my cock deep inside of you?"

"Yes...I mean...no," she stammers nervously, "I just... I've never...No one has ever talked to me like this before."

"That's a shame."

"Why do you say that?" Her question comes as I take the steps onto the patio.

"Because," I lower her to the ground and slide my finger along her slick cunt, "it's quite obvious that you enjoy it."

She visibly startles and her cheeks pinken at the sound of a deep chuckle. I hadn't seen Eduardo and Andres sitting at the table at the other side of the patio. But from their vantage point, they had seen plenty.

"What the fuck are you doing at my place?" My tone is gruff, angered that their presence has obviously embarrassed Izzy.

My reaction catches them off-guard, as I normally don't give a shit who sees the whores I fuck.

But Izzy isn't just some whore I want to put my cock in and send home.

I didn't spend the night with her at the bar to bring her back to my place and fuck her. I spent hours with her because I am thoroughly enjoying her company.

Fucking her tonight is going to be an unexpected bonus.

"We had a...a...business thing come up," Eduardo stammers while quickly standing from the table.

"That didn't answer my question," I feel my jaw flex uncontrollably as my brows furrow.

Realizing that I'm mad as hell at being interrupted, Andres promptly stands as well and sputters, "A situation came up from the meeting earlier."

"Then why are you here?" My tone is becoming increasingly agitated, "Are you not capable of dealing with it on your own? I'm pretty sure I literally pay you to deal with situations."

"We can handle it," Eduardo's eyes dart between Andres and me.

"Yeah," Andres nervously nods in agreement, "We can handle it."

"I should...um...I should go." Izzy's voice is quiet beside me.

"Then get the fuck out," my voice is firm and deep.

Feeling Izzy step from beside me, my hand firmly grips her wrist as Eduardo and Andres quickly make their way toward the stairs.

"I think you're forgetting something," my head motions toward Izzy and I loosen the grip I have on her wrist..

"I'm sorry ma'am," Eduardo's tone is shaky, yet sincere, as he apologizes. "I'm sorry we interrupted your evening, boss."

Giving a quick nod of my head, the two of them quickly take the stairs and disappear down the beach.

"I didn't know they were here," I place my finger under her chin and tip her head up so I can look into her eyes, "I assure you; we won't be interrupted again. I apologize for their behavior and inadvertently putting you in that situation, but if you want to leave, I understand."

four

ISABELLA

"So, they work for you?" I question.

Knowing it breaks the rules we established earlier tonight at the bar, I'm surprised when he answers, "Yes. We are all down here for a business meeting."

"Are you sure you don't need to deal with whatever it was they were here for?"

"They've worked for me for a long time. They are more than capable of dealing with whatever the issue is," Alex crosses the patio to where the two guys were sitting. Turning back toward me, he lifts a bottle of tequila from the table.

"A small one," I smile, "Maybe a half shot."

I'm already alone with a man I don't know at a foreign resort, being drunk as well is probably not the best of ideas.

As he turns back to the table to pour the drinks, I slowly meander the patio as I walk toward him. My eyes take in the luxurious outdoor furniture and well-maintained plants that provide a great deal of privacy while still granting the view of the ocean below.

"The patio of your villa is about five times larger than my whole hotel room. How much does a place like this cost?" My hand slaps over my mouth, "I'm sorry, that was rude."

I am relieved when he smiles at me instead of being offended, "Similar villas on the property run about eighty-five hundred dollars."

"A week? That's crazy!"

"A night," he replies, and I feel my jaw drop, "This is my personal villa though, and it does not get rented out by the resort."

"You *own* an eight thousand dollar a night villa?"

"I travel here often, and I like knowing it's always available."

Alex turns from the table and steps closer to me. I notice that he only has one shot glass in his hand, and it is not a small shot.

"That's way more of a shot than I wanted," I look at the glass full to the brim.

"This isn't all for you *cerecita*," his hand lightly grips my jaw and tilts my head up before he continues, "Now, open those pretty pink lips for me."

Parting my lips, I watch as he lifts the glass to his. He bends down slowly and his lips hover above mine. I feel the warm liquid dribble on my lips, dripping both down my chin and into my mouth.

Why is this man essentially spitting tequila in my mouth hot as fuck?

His lips press into mine and his warm, tequila-coated tongue explores the inside of my mouth. Pulling back from the kiss, I am breathless when he slowly licks the remaining tequila from my chin and neck.

I don't know if it's the tequila, his kiss, or my brain telling me that Mexico is like a tropical version of Vegas...but I suddenly don't care what happened between the beach and this moment...

As his lips kiss along my collarbone, his large hands grip the backs of my thighs. He lifts me effortlessly and my legs instinctively wrap around his waist.

"Your salty skin goes amazing with this tequila," his words vibrate against my neck as he carries me to the outdoor shower. After turning it on, he tucks a stray tendril of hair behind my ear, "but I'm thinking we rinse off the ocean and sand before heading inside."

With one hand under my ass and the other roaming my back, he carries me into the shower. I can feel Alex undoing the strings holding my bikini top in place. Lowering me to the ground under the stream of water, he pulls the loosened top over my head.

Both of his hands are immediately on my breasts, squeezing them firmly while rolling my nipples. The fingertips teasing my nipples are replaced by his mouth, and I'm unable to contain my moans when he sucks gently and flicks it with his tongue. His mouth wanders my chest, covering my breasts with wet kisses and tender bites. Through the kisses, he urges me backward until my back is pressed against the smooth stone wall.

The kisses slowly make their way down my stomach as he kneels, until he is kissing at the fabric of my bikini bottoms. Looking down at him, I am surprised to find his sparkling blue eyes staring up at me as his fingers slip under the strings of my bikini. The intimacy of his gaze causes me to avert my eyes.

"Does it make you uncomfortable?" His tone is sincere as he pulls my bottoms over my hips and down my thighs, "That I enjoy watching your pleasure?"

"No, I...," my words cut short as his tongue slides through the slit of my pussy.

"Good," his hand slides along my thigh. Lifting it, he hooks my knee over his shoulder and places another long hard lick against my center that causes my body to shudder.

"Now be a good girl and watch me," his lips vibrate against my clit, "Watch how much I enjoy your delicious cunt."

Turning my eyes back to him, our gazes lock. I watch his tongue slowly slide through me, causing my breath to tremble while I chew on my bottom lip.

"You like watching," he raises an eyebrow, "don't you?"

"Yes," the word comes out of me as a whispered moan.

"Ride my face. Grind those curvy hips all over my tongue until you come," his hands grip my ass as he moves me over his tongue, "I want you to see what destroying you does to me."

His hands continue to work me over his mouth until I begin to make my own rhythm, chasing that same electric surge I felt with his fingers inside of me. My back arches as my hips steadily roll over his tongue, my body begins to quiver, and my breathy whimpers become quiet screams.

I do as he asked. My eyes watching him while his tongue glides continuously over my clit. I watch as his face grows more needy. The eyes staring back up at me more lustful by the minute.

I need more...

My fingers lace through his hair, fisting it tightly and pulling him against me with force. His face winces and he moans into my skin, but the look on his face isn't one of physical pain.

His moan nearly pushes me over the edge. My hips grind harder and faster, while I use the grip of his hair to move him to exactly where I need him.

"Yes," I scream, and he groans hard against me as though he is the one experiencing my pleasure. The vibration of his moan on my clit does me in, and I come with his face buried between my thighs.

When I finally release the tight grip I held on his hair, he smiles and licks his lips when he sits back from me. Sliding my leg from his shoulder, he places kisses up my stomach as he slowly stands before me.

"Do you have any idea how fucking delicious your sweet little cunt is when it creams all over my face?"

Not knowing quite how to answer, I just shake my head at him.

"Do you want to? Do you want to know how sweet you taste?"

His question intrigues me.

"Yes," I embarrassingly whisper.

"Such a dirty little girl," he whispers back before his lips crash against mine. The tangy taste of my own arousal fills my mouth and I groan into his mouth as he lifts me from the ground.

Our tongues sharing the taste of my pussy, Alex carries me into the house. Expecting him to take me into the bedroom, I am surprised when he places my ass on a table in the hallway.

"Sorry, *cerecita*," he groans as he drops to his knees before me and presses my thighs apart, "but I need more of you."

Did this man just apologize because he wants to eat my pussy again?

Out of my previous partners, only one has ever gone down on me. He didn't enjoy it, and it felt like it only happened out of obligation in an attempt to make me wet.

Not Alex...

His mouth licks and sucks at me like I'm the most delicious meal he's ever eaten.

"Fuck," I groan as he brings me to the edge, only to stop and kiss the tender skin of my upper thighs.

five

ALEJANDRO

She tastes like fucking Heaven.

Hearing her groans when I edge her causes me to smile as I nip at her thighs, "Such a greedy little girl. So eager to come again."

"And you're such a tease," she snips back at me.

"If you want me to actually tease you," my tongue flicks over her clit before returning to her thighs, "I can show you what that's actually like."

"I thought you brought me here," her words breathy as I suck a tender spot on her inner thigh, "to worship me."

God damn.

It isn't often, or ever, that a woman puts me in my place like that.

"Well," my hand firmly grips her thigh as I smirk up at her, "I am nothing, if not a man of my word."

Before she has a chance to say anything, my tongue is on her clit and two of my fingers are pressing inside of her. Sucking her into my mouth as my fingers curl and thrust inside of her, I watch as her whole body arches.

Groaning against her clit, my cock is throbbing in my shorts. The wet shorts are so tight and heavy, they feel painfully restricting.

Or my cock just wants out of these cold, wet shorts and into her warm, wet cunt.

My tongue and fingers work her in tandem, she is so close to coming. Her tits rise and fall with every heavy breath and moan coming from her. The arousal from her cunt is running down my fucking arm. I can feel her walls beginning to tighten around my fingers. But none of it compares to that lusty look of pure pleasure in her eyes.

What man wouldn't give his time and dedication to watching this woman come?

I can't fucking get enough of her.

Ready to burst myself from her sheer arousal, a grumbly moan rises from my chest over her clit. It's what does her in. Her fingers grip the edge of the table, and her heels dig into my back, screams of pleasure coming from her as her hips writhe against my face.

I stand and shed my shorts the moment she comes down from her release. My lips on hers and my tongue swirling her arousal around her mouth, I aggressively lift her from the table and carry her to the bedroom.

I need to be inside of her.

We crash through the bedroom door, and I lay her on the bed. Quickly pulling a condom from the bedside table, I tear it open with my teeth and roll it down my length. Her eyes are wide and her expression is nervous as she watches me.

"Are you sure you want to do this?" I slowly climb over her body.

"Yes," her voice expresses the same anxiety as her face, "I'm sure."

"You don't sound sure."

"I knew it was big," her eyes dart between us to my cock currently resting on her stomach, "when I grabbed it earlier. Just..."

"With how fucking wet you are," I lift my hips to position myself against her entrance, "you'll have no problem taking me."

Pressing the tip into her, I still for a moment giving her time to realize that I won't hurt her. She hugs every last inch of me as I slide inside of her. "Fuck," I groan into her neck, "Your tight cunt feels so good stretching around my cock."

Rolling my hips, slowly, I begin to thrust in and out of her.

She moans and her hands grip my shoulders.

"Fuck, *cerecita*," I pull her hands above her head and pin her to the bed, "You're making me not want to be gentle with you."

"Don't be," her hips lift from the bed to meet mine as she begs with breathy words, "Please. Don't hold back."

Is it that obvious I'm fighting the need to totally overpower her?

Lifting my hips and pulling nearly all my length from her, she lets out a gasp when I drive myself into her hard and deep.

"Yes," she moans as I repeat the motion.

Using one of my hands to hold hers above her head, the other bruisingly grips her hip as I relentlessly drive into her. Fighting against my firm hold, her back arches from the bed and her legs clutch around my hips.

"You wanted it hard," I grunt out the words between thrusts, "Now fucking come for me."

When she does as she's told, clenching around my cock and screaming out my name, I nearly lose control.

Sitting up onto my feet between her legs, I pull myself from her and flip her onto her stomach. My arm tugs under her hips, lifting her ass into the air before sliding back into her.

My eyes stare at where the two of us meet, watching her cunt continue to swallow my cock. Her perfect round ass jiggling with every thrust, just waiting to be spanked.

When my palm strikes the fleshy curve of her ass, she groans and pushes her hips back into me. Spanking her again, her hands claw at the sheets in front of her.

My fingers slide into the hair at the back of her head. Fisting it, she moans when I pull her head back. Using her bright-red locks to pull her face toward me, I bend over her and take her mouth with the same aggression that I am using to thrust into her cunt. Both of us groan into each other's mouths.

"I can't fucking get enough of you," my hips grind against her ass as she begins whimpering, quickly working toward another release.

"Am I going to get the pleasure of watching you come again?" I groan while fighting back my own orgasm. "Show me again how beautiful you are as you milk my fucking cock."

Her mouth opens, but only a silent scream comes from it. When she clenches around me so hard that I can feel her thighs trembling, it is my undoing. My balls tighten and I can no longer hold back. My cock spasms, and with a primal grunt, I fill the condom, wishing desperately that I was unloading into her.

Collapsing on top of her, my lips kiss over the soft skin of her shoulders as I pull myself from her and climb from the bed, "I'll be right back, *cerecita.*"

six

ISABELLA

So exhausted that I can barely lift my head, I watch his tight ass as he walks to the bathroom to dispose of the condom. Alex is gone only a minute before he returns to the doorway. My eyes scan over him, in awe that his body is almost perfection.

"Needy for more already," he smirks at me when he catches me eyeing him over.

Climbing back into the bed, he slides my body into his while pulling the sheets over the two of us. Holding me in his arms, his fingers slowly rake through my hair.

"You know that I'm here for business," he continues to play with my curls, "What is it that brings you to Mexico by yourself?"

Rolling onto my stomach, I lay my arms on his chest and rest my chin on them, "Is this a trick to find out if anyone will miss me before you traffic me?"

"Yes," he smirks back at me, "I absolutely hate loose ends."

"Short or long version?"

"Long version."

"After college, I moved to New York City when I took a job with Amica Publishing," I pause when I realize my mistake, "Shit!"

This man has literally seen my asshole, I think he can know where I live.

"Fuck it. My name is Isabella Drake, but my friends all call me Izzy. I'm twenty-six years old and I live in New York City."

Please care, at least a little?

"Nice to meet you Isabella Drake from New York City," he lifts his head and kisses my lips. "Now tell me, what brought you to Mexico?"

"Work was going amazing. I was getting comfortable in the city. I met Ian," I watch as his brow furrows a little, "And then my best friend from back college moved in with me about two months ago."

"So, you're down here by yourself because? Your boyfriend and your best friend weren't available?"

"I'm getting to it. Last week, Amica laid off half of their staff. I was part of that half. I wound up going home much earlier than usual, and I walked in on Courtney riding Ian like she was at the rodeo. I locked myself in my room and cried for a few days about my whole life going to shit in the span of a few hours. Figuring I didn't have much to lose, except my financial responsibility," I shrug, "I maxed out my credit card and booked myself a weeklong trip here."

"That's rough, *cerecita*," his fingers rub along my jaw, "On the bright side, you got him out of your life before it got serious, and now your so-called friend is stuck with that inability-to-give-an-orgasm dick."

"So," I continue after I finish laughing at his comment, "When I fly back tomorrow, I need to figure out what I'm doing with my life...starting by finding a new place to live. Your turn."

"My turn?" he questions back at me.

"I told you about me..."

"So, you just expect me to break the rules of our game and tell you all about me?"

"Seriously?" I lift my head off my arms, the look on my face apparently showing my feelings.

Grabbing my waist, he pulls me on top of him. Still annoyed that he blew off my request to know more about him, I sit up. Not realizing that this leaves me straddling him.

"I'm kidding," his hands run along my back as he pulls me back down to his chest, "What do you want to know?"

"Your name?" I ask as I lay on his chest, my legs straddling his waist.

"Alex," I can hear him smirking as he pauses trying to rile me up, before his deep voice replies, "My name is Alejandro Marcano."

"How old are you?"

"How old do you think I am?" He counters my question.

Lifting myself a little from his chest, I stroke at the hair by his temples, "This tells me you're older, but you also look better without a shirt on than any guy I've ever met in person."

"I think I'm going to take that as a compliment," he smirks up at me, "I'm forty-two."

Thank God!

Not older than my dad!

"Where do you live?"

"New York City," I try to hide my girlish smile as he replies.

"So, I know you're down here for a business trip," I continue my questioning, "What is it that you do?"

"Quite a few things," he responds, "but I primarily facilitate the travel of goods between countries."

"And that pays this well?"

Shit! I did it again?

"I own the company," he pushes my hair behind my ear, "Marcano Enterprises."

"You're *that* Alejandro Marcano?"

No big deal...

I just fucked a billionaire, who also happens to be New York City's most eligible bachelor.

While I'd never seen a picture of him, he is the talk of single women throughout the city. A hot as hell, rich as fuck, eligible bachelor. The things women would do just for a chance to meet this man.

The things they would do if they knew he also fucked like a porn star...

"Is that a problem?" His tone has a tinge of concern to it.

"I mean...no...," I stammer, "Why didn't you say anything?"

"It was refreshing to meet an amazing woman that had absolutely no idea who I was for a change," his fingers trail along my back, "What else do you want to know about me?"

Laying with him, we continue to talk for hours. The conversation is as comfortable and easy as it was when tequila was free-flowing at the bar.

Lifting my head, my eyes catch a glimpse of the alarm clock. It's four in the morning. Climbing off Alex, I slide from the bed.

"Where do you think you're going?" His voice is gravelly, and he is noticeably miffed.

"I need to go," I try to remember where my clothes are, "My flight leaves in a few hours and I still need to pack up my room. I can't afford to miss my flight."

"Stay," he wraps his arms around me from behind and pulls me against his body. I immediately feel his hard cock pressed against my lower back and his lips on my neck. "I'll make sure you get home, eventually."

SEVEN

ISABELLA

Excluding the brief period of time that we both fell asleep, out of sheer exhaustion, Alex hasn't kept his hands off me since I tried to leave early this morning.

At this point, I'm pretty sure he's trying to help me make up for all the orgasmless sex I've been having until now.

It's nearly noon when I finally leave Alex's villa to pack up my things, doing the ultimate walk of shame. Yet I don't feel embarrassed as I walk the hotel in a pair of his boxer briefs and a button-down shirt that fits me like a dress, while carrying my still sopping wet bathing suit in my hand.

Swiping my keycard, I head into my room and grab my phone from the nightstand. Fifteen text messages.

IAN

Baby it's been 4 days

Talk to me

I'm sorry

It was just that one time

You know I love you

It'll never happen again

Izzy?

Please answer me

No one has heard from you in days

I'm worried

COURTNEY

Izzy please come back to the apartment

I want to explain

I'm sorry

It was stupid

I feel horrible.

Tossing my phone on the bed, I grab my suitcase and a laundry bag from the closet. Shoving my wet suit in the bag, I sling it into my suitcase. Grabbing a pair of jeans and a white t-shirt, I change out of Alex's clothes. Not knowing what to do with them, I decide to pack it in my bag with the rest of my things.

I guess I'll get it back to him at some point.

Just as I'm finishing, there's a knock at the door.

"Miss," he knocks again, "Mr. Marcano sent me to collect you and your belongings."

Collect my belongings? Who says that?

Opening the door, Andres is standing in the hallway. Unlike his scruffy attire last night, today he is in dress slacks and a button-up shirt. The only thing marring his perfect appearance is the large bruise running along his left jaw.

Allowing him in, he looks surprised, "Just the one bag?"

"Yes."

"He got stuck on a business call and he's going to meet us in the lobby," he grabs my suitcase, "Are you ready to go?"

Taking a quick look around the room to ensure I didn't forget anything, I nod at him and he heads to the door to call the elevator. When it arrives, we both step inside. It is silent when the doors close.

"This isn't going to be like that Claire Dane's movie," I begin talking of the first thing I think of, "You know, *Brokedown Palace*?"

"Miss?" He fidgets as though I have suddenly made him uncomfortable.

"You know? Girl meets guy on tropical vacation. Guy puts drugs in her bag, and she winds up spending years in some foreign prison."

"No," he can't leave the elevator fast enough when it opens at the lobby.

Apparently he's never seen the movie.

He walks directly to Alex, who is sitting in one of the plush chairs by reception, and whispers something in his ear. Alex glances at me and chuckles before returning his attention to Andres, "Get the car and we'll meet you out front."

Standing from his chair, Alex looks impeccable. He is wearing a pair of very well-tailored, dark navy trousers and a white, button-up, shirt – all of which accentuates the physique I know it is covering.

How am I so underdressed for the airport?

He walks to me and takes my tote bag before kissing the side of my neck.

Oh. We're still doing that?

The lines of this one night stand are a little fuzzy with him buying me a flight home and all.

"You ready to go?" He places his hand on the small of my back and leads me outside to where Andres is waiting with the car.

"Eduardo is waiting for us at the airport, sir," Andres opens the door for the two of us, "He said everything has been taken care of."

"Thank you," Alex guides me into the car and then slides in beside me.

A few minutes into our ride, Alex places his hand on my knee and slowly slides it up my thigh. His hands on my body immediately bring back memories of just how good his hands on me feel.

"It's a shame you wore jeans," his hand travels the rest of my thigh and firmly grips my pussy, causing me to gasp.

His hand, still rubbing hard against me, my breaths get raspy as he works me closer and closer to an orgasm through my pants. As my hips begin rocking to meet his rough touch, he leans down to my ear and gravelly whispers, "I was planning to fuck you on the way the airport."

His lips travel my neck and he brings me closer and closer to the edge.

"And that isn't nearly as much fun when you're in pants," his lips kiss over the fabric of the shirt covering my breasts.

Trying to be quiet with Andres on the other side of the car's divider, I bite my lip and quiet moans come from my mouth.

"You're so fucking close," he growls into my ear before patting my pussy and putting his hand back on my knee. "Too bad that now we're both going to have to wait until we're on the plane."

Fuck.

I squirm in my seat, my body needing the release he just denied me.

"I am not joining the Mile High Club in some tiny, dirty airplane bathroom," my words still breathy, as I try to regain my composure.

"I would never ask you to do such a thing, *cerecita*," he finishes when the car comes to a stop.

Andres cracks the divider, "We're here, sir. Are you ready to board?"

"Yes," he looks at me for a moment as he slides his hand back up my thigh, "I think we're more than ready."

A moment later my door opens. Stepping out, I realize that we are not at the airport. At least not the airport I used when I flew into Mexico. Turning back to face Alex, I notice that there is a large plane with the words *Marcano Enterprises* written by the tail.

Closing the distance between us, Alex leans back down to my ear, "But I do intend to have you join the Mile High Club to help me christen my new plane."

eight

ALEJANDRO

"Alex," Izzy exclaims as she steps onto the plane behind me, "This is not a plane. This is a fucking house that flies."

Eduardo and Andres sit on the couch while doing their best to stifle their laughs, even though they don't do a good job.

I sit in one of the lounge chairs and Izzy attempts to walk past me to take the one next to me. As she does, I grab her waist and pull her into the gap between my thighs, "I would prefer if you sat with me."

She doesn't argue and gets comfortable curled up on my lap. Rubbing my hand along her thigh, she is asleep before we finish taxiing to the runway.

The three of us discuss the reason they came to my villa last night while Izzy sleeps peacefully resting against me. After about an hour, I am fully caught up on the events of the evening, and certain that they handled things accordingly. We spend another hour discussing a few upcoming items for this week before finishing up with business.

"She hasn't moved. You apparently wore her the fuck out last night," Eduardo razzes me as though we are teenagers in the locker room.

"Watch your fucking mouth," my tone is sharp but quiet as to not wake Izzy, "That's twice in less than twelve hours you've disrespected her."

"I don't see the big deal," I watch as Andres elbows Eduardo, silently telling him to shut his mouth, "She's just some whore you picked up at the res-"

Clenching my jaw, I nod my head at Andres. Lifting his arm, he places a firm elbow to Eduardo's face, breaking his nose.

"Not a fucking word," I seethe through my teeth while stroking Izzy's hair, "If I hear a sound out of you the rest of this flight, you'll have the opportunity to learn if you can fly at thirty fucking thousand feet."

Holding his face and fighting the urge to cry out in pain, he nods his head at me.

"Disrespect her again, and I'll carve your fucking tongue from your mouth myself. Understood?"

With a tinge of fear in his eyes, he nods his head at me. When I told Izzy last night that I was a man of my word, I meant it. The men that work for me know it too. I don't give idle threats.

"Andres, go help him clean up his fucking face," the two of them stand from the couch. When Andres extends an arm to help Eduardo he bumps past him, trying to maintain what little control he has. "And close the partition."

The sound of the partition clicking shut causes Izzy to stir in her sleep. While it doesn't fully wake her, she also is no longer fully asleep.

When my lips press against her neck, she leans into my touch. Kissing down her neck, I can feel the pulse beating under my lips gradually getting faster. Her eyelids flutter when my lips make their way back to her jaw.

"Alex," her voice is groggy, "How long was I asleep?"

"Too long," I continue to kiss along her jaw toward her, "but I think it's time you wake up so we can finish what we started in the car."

She leans harder into my lips and moans softly. As she wakes and becomes more aware of her surroundings, she startles and spins her head around.

"They aren't here," I gently grab her face and turn her head back to me, "I told you. That is not a situation I would put you in on purpose."

My hand slides between her thighs and grips her cunt. Firmly massaging her through her jeans, she is quickly writhing on my lap. "They aren't worthy of seeing you like that or watching your pleasure. No man is, except for me!"

Continuing to rub against her with one hand, my other undoes the button of her jeans. Yanking the waistband, the zipper falls, and I squeeze my hand into her tight jeans. They are so tight that I can't get my fingers inside of her like I want. My fingers rub over her clit, and she quickly gets to the brink.

"No man except for me," I groan into her ear, while rolling her clit between my fingers, "Now, come for me, *cerecita*."

My mouth covers hers, swallowing her screams as she continues to rock her hips into my touch as she rides out her orgasm.

Pulling my hand from her pants, I firmly grip her waist and stand her from my lap. I grab her jeans and pull them over her hips, taking her underwear with them. Unbuckling my pants, I stand from my seat and stroke my already hard cock through my boxer briefs.

"I had planned to spend a little more time torturing and pleasuring you," I pull the condom from my pocket. Freeing my cock, I roll it on before spinning Izzy around and forcefully pressing her face down on the table. She lets out a loud grunt, her body falling flush with the table as I shove the entirety of myself inside of her.

"We're almost in New York," I grip her hips firmly with both hands and bury my cock inside of her, "I'm going to take you hard and fast so that we can come before we land."

With both of us nearly fully clothed, I plow into her from behind. Her hands firmly gripping the table and her hips pressing back into every thrust.

"Does my dirty little girl like being bent over and fucked from behind?"

"Yes," she groans against the table.

"When I fuck your tight little cunt from behind," my fingertips dig into her ass cheeks and slightly pull them apart, "I wonder what it would be like to stretch out that tight little virgin ass of yours."

I gather the saliva in my mouth and I spit it against her virgin hole. Watching it clench as my spit slides over it, she moans and my cock twitches inside of her cunt.

"Fuck, *cerecita*," I groan fighting desperately not to come, slowing my thrusts to regain my composure.

Sliding my hand around her hip, I rub her clit with my fingertips while burying myself inside of her again.

"I want to fuck that tight little hole and fill it with my cum," the words sound savage coming from my mouth, "I want to fill every last one of your holes with my cum."

Never in my life have I wanted to fuck a woman bare, but damn the consequences, I want to fill this one with my seed.

"Fuck you day and night," I feel her clench around me, "until I'm literally dripping from you."

"Fuck, Alex," her hands grip the table so tightly when she comes that her knuckles turn white, "Yes. I want to feel you pump your cum into me."

There is no stopping what her words do to me. My hips stutter against her ass. I fill the condom, roaring loudly as I come with a ferocity I have never felt before.

Pulling myself from her, I remove the condom and tuck myself back into my boxers. Leaning over her, my hands roam her body as lips kiss down her spine. I bend down and grab her panties, pulling them back up her legs and over her hips. She stands unsteadily, and I pull her jeans up. Working them over her curvy hips, I raise the zipper and do the button when I stand.

Tucking her tousled hair behind her ears, I cup her face in my hands and pull her in for a kiss. Lifting her into my arms, I carry her to the couch and sit with her on my lap. Her tired body is slumped against my still heaving chest.

I cannot fucking get enough of her.

nine

ISABELLA

A resort villa that costs more per night than I make in a month.

A flying fucking house.

And now I'm in a car that probably costs as much as my parents' house.

And all of it with a man that no less than an hour ago, I actually told to "pump me full of cum."

Who fucking says that?

The previously blurred lines of this supposed one night stand aren't even lines anymore...

While I had already requested an Uber to take me to my apartment, Alex was adamant that he would drive me. He refused to take no for an answer. As he makes his way through the city streets, his right arm rests on the console and his fingers occasionally stroke along my outer thigh.

"Up here on the right," I gesture toward my building and Alex pulls into an open spot out front. Ever the gentleman, he opens my door, helps me from the car, and is determined to carry my suitcase up to my apartment.

Reaching my apartment, I pull my keys from my purse and put them into the door. As I unlock the door and slowly push it open, Alex's lips are the side of my neck. Walking me into the apartment, his fingers dip into the top of my jeans and he growls, "I want to taste you again, before I go."

"Izz?" I'm startled by Ian's voice coming from the couch. Less startled by the fact that Courtney is laying on his lap.

"Who the fuck is this guy?" Ian abruptly stands from the couch. Courtney just stares at me in silence.

I think she realized when I never responded that our friendship was pretty much over.

Pulling his hand from the front of my pants, Alex extends his hand to Ian, "I'm Alex. You must be Ethan."

"Ian," he curtly corrects him and declines shaking his hand, "What the fuck, Izz? You disappear for a fucking week only to show back up with this guy shoving his hands in your pants?"

"Considering a week ago, I walked in on you fucking Courtney, I don't really see how any of that is your business," I take a couple of steps to my room, only to be stopped when a firm hand grips painfully around my wrist.

"Ouch, Ian," I cry out as I wince, "You're hurting me."

"You fucking whore," Ian spits, "You're fucking him, aren't you?"

Before I have a chance to respond, Alex has gripped the front of Ian's shirt with both hands and has him pinned against the wall. I watch Alex's nostrils flare, the vile hatred written across his face, standing mere inches from Ian.

"Don't...fucking...touch...her," Alex seethes through his teeth.

"Get the fuck off me, man!" Ian yells, a tinge of fear in his voice, as he tries to fight against Alex's hold.

Leaning his face even closer, Alex's words are quieter but equally as irate, "And don't you even think about fucking talking to her like that again."

"Get what you need, *cerecita*," Alex's words are softer toward me as he continues to press Ian to the wall, "I'm not leaving you here with this piece of shit."

Ian has never laid a hand on me like that before, but I also don't want to stick around to see if he'll do it again. In my room, I quickly shove some of my clothes into a duffel bag. When I return to the living room, Alex still has Ian pinned to the wall. Alex is leaning in and quietly saying something, to which Ian looks terrified.

Alex decreases the distance between the two of them, "Do we have an understanding?"

Ian merely rapidly nods his head to answer.

"Good boy, Ethan," Alex firmly taps his hand twice against Ian's face.

"Are you ready?" He turns to me while pulling his wallet from his pants.

"Yes," I nod my head at him.

Courtney still sits on the couch, refusing to make eye contact with me. Alex walks to the table in front of her and drops a wad of money, "That should cover Isabella's portion of the rent until the lease is up. Someone will be by to get her things."

Taking the duffel bag from me and grabbing the suitcase, he puts his free hand on the small of my back and guides me from the apartment.

I manage to contain myself until we are outside of the building. But once we step out onto the city streets, I am completely overwhelmed with emotions and unable to contain my tears any longer. They flow down my face.

"What the hell am I going to do?" I cry out as Alex pulls me against his chest.

"Shhhhh," Alex wraps his arms tightly around me and strokes my hair. "Everything is going to be fine."

"How can you say that?" My cascading tears dampen his shirt, "I can't stay here. I have nowhere to go. And I barely have enough money to make a deposit on a new place. I'm going to wind up back in Connecticut with my parents."

"Get in the car," his voice firm, yet tender, "you have somewhere to go."

ten

ALEJANDRO

The majority of the time I spent meeting with Eduardo and Andres on the flight was occupied running through various scenarios of what to do with Isabella. More correctly, how to get her to come home with me instead of leaving her at the apartment with her ex-boyfriend and former best friend.

When I heard two voices on the other side of the door, Ian and Courtney pretty much took care of that for me. I knew there was no way in hell she was staying with the people who continued to betray her. She deserves better than that.

She will get better than that.

My control almost went out the window when Ian dared to lay a hand on her, let alone when she cried out because he had hurt her. I could have fucking gutted him. After my conversation with that little limp-dick, it is very unlikely he will ever lay a hand on another woman again. He will definitely never dare to even look at Isabella ever again.

At least, that is assuming he wants to keep that useless cock between his legs.

Isabella might not realize it now, but I'm taking her exactly where she was going to wind up anyway.

I want her with me.

And I always get what I fucking want.

Turning toward her when we stop at a traffic light, I notice she still has the remnants of her tears on her face. Using my thumb, I gently wipe the wet, smudged mascara from her cheeks.

"Alex?" There is a tremble in her voice, and she hesitates to continue.

"I've got you *cerecita*," I place my hand on her thigh and grip it lightly before turning my eyes back to the road as traffic begins to move again, "I'm going to make sure you are well taken care of."

"I can't ask you to do that."

"You aren't asking," my thumb caresses her thigh and I tighten my grip, "I'm telling you."

"But, Alex?" Her voice trembles again.

In the short time I've known her, I know more about Isabella than any woman that has come before her. I never really cared to know any of them. They didn't interest me intellectually. The desire to talk to them, to learn more about them, had never been present. They were nothing more than a hole to fuck.

The idea of fucking Isabella had definitely crossed my mind. It was what originally enticed me to sit next to her at the bar. I enjoyed talking with her, actually talking and getting to know her. She is so different from any woman I've met before. She's pure, untarnished by the world that I live in. Her innocent heart reminds me that there is good in this evil world I have built for myself, and maybe that there is even a little good left in me.

"I want to take care of you," the tone in my voice is sincere.

I mean every word coming from my mouth.

Shaking her head as she looks at me, "You don't even know me."

"I know more than enough."

Reaching my place, I pull the car into the garage and park. I stay silent and get out of the car to give her a moment to finish her thoughts.

She looks up at me when I open her door to help her from the car, hesitating for a moment before climbing from her seat and standing beside me.

At her rightful place, by my side.

"Wait," she grabs my arm as we walk toward the elevator, "My bags. We didn't get them from the car."

"One of the guys will ensure your stuff is brought upstairs. Let me have your keys."

"My keys?" She pulls them from her purse and hands them to me with a questioning look on her face. The slightly confused look only intensifies when she sees the two men flanking the waiting elevator.

"I'll text you," I hand her keys to the guard standing on my left, "and let you know what to do with these."

"Come," I usher Isabella into the elevator. I push the button for the penthouse and turn to face her, "I will send one of my men to go get the rest of your things from the apartment."

"One of the guys that works for you?" She looks up at me with a disagreeable look on her face, "I don't want some guy packing up my personal things. Going through and touching all of my...stuff."

The doors open, granting us access directly to my penthouse apartment. Placing my hand on the small of her back, I lead her from the elevator and into the main living area. Her eyes widen as she takes in the space.

"It's an expression. I have women that work for me too," my fingers slide under her chin, "Do you really think I would let some other man put his hands on your panties?"

"You think that by staying here, it means you get to decide who does and doesn't get to touch my panties?"

"Oh, *cerecita*," I pull her body flush against mine and smirk down at her, "What makes you think it has anything to do with staying with me?"

eleven

ISABELLA

Every time Alex puts his hands on me or pulls me against his body, it's as though I lose any ability to form a logical thought.

Or keep my panties on.

His hand slides down my back to my waist. My breath stutters when I feel his fingers dip inside the waistband as he slowly slides his hands to the button of my jeans.

"Alex…" I can barely muster his name, my body already so needy for what he provides.

His lips press against mine as I place my hands on his chest. I am about to push myself away from him when his lips travel to my ear.

"Do you want to see your new home, *cerecita*?" The words are breathy as he whispers them in my ear.

His fingers pop the button of my jeans, and he continues to whisper in my ear, "Do you want to see it before or after I fuck you in it?"

As I am about to answer, his hand slides under the thin fabric of my panties. Squeezing his large hand into my tight jeans, he goes straight for my entrance and I feel his fingertips swirl around it.

"So fucking wet for me," his finger slides through my slit, "Always so eager to be fucked by me."

Pulling his hand free, he grips my jeans with both hands and begins pulling them down my legs causing the rate of my breathing to continue to grow faster. Reaching my feet, he bends to undo the straps of both my sandals before removing them from my feet. Alex slowly pulls each of the pant legs over my feet before tossing the jeans to the floor.

Kneeling before me, his fingertips slowly dust along my skin from my ankles up to my hips as his lips brush along my inner thighs. He is savoring each touch nearly as much as I am.

"Tell me, *cerecita*," the back of his hand drags along the front of my panties causing me to groan with need, "Do other men make you this wet and needy? Or is this how your pussy reacts just for me?"

"You," I moan as his fingers rub my clit through my panties, "Only you."

It's not a lie...

I've struggled to be physically aroused with my previous partners, yet it happens at the mere thought of Alex touching me.

"Tell me," His finger slides under the front of my panties, pulling them to the side and exposing me to him. His tongue licks over my clit, "That's because this is my sweet cunt."

Hovering his face so close between my upper thighs that I can feel his expelled breath blowing over my clit, his words blow against my skin, "Is it mine, *cerecita*?"

His lips on my skin, his eyes look up toward my face. While his fingers continue to dance over the skin of my hips and thighs, he stares at me. Patiently waiting for me to answer him.

I don't know how to respond.

"Don't think about it," his mouth gently sucks the skin of my inner thigh, "Do you want me to fuck and pleasure your cunt as I please?"

"Yes," the lone word leaves me as though I'm begging for my life.

"Then tell me it's mine," his lips and breaths dust over the bare skin of my pussy and thighs as he continues to toy with my desperate need for him.

"It's...it's yours," I struggle out the words when his tongue teasingly licks through my slit and he momentarily sucks my clit into his mouth.

"Such a good girl," he growls along the skin of my stomach as he stands. Pulling my shirt over my head, he tosses it to the floor with my pants. His lips on my neck, he slowly readjusts the strap of my bra, situating it back on my shoulder.

I guess at least this time I've managed to keep my panties.

"Now," he hooks his finger under the front of my panties and pulls them back into place, covering me, "Let me show you around."

Taking my hand, he begins walking further into the apartment. Nearly naked, my bare feet pad on the hardwood floors behind him as I follow his lead into the apartment.

In comparison, the apartment we just left may as well have been a cardboard box.

This place is massive. The main living area is all an open floor concept. The windows are so broad, that the dark hardwood floors almost look like they travel straight out into the city skyline. Nearly all of the furniture is black wood or leather. It's beautifully decorated and looks like it fell from a magazine, but it also quite clearly the home of a bachelor.

Pulling me past the sleek, black leather chaise, Alex walks me into the kitchen. The black cabinets fill the space to the ceiling, but the whole room is lightened by the white marble counters that also run up the wall like backsplash.

Alex's large hands grip my waist, and he hoists me onto the kitchen island. Before I can finish gasping, he has stepped between my knees.

twelve

ALEJANDRO

"Wait," she firmly plants both of her hands on my chest.

Gripping her ass, I pull her to the edge of the counter. Leaning into her hands, I ensure she can feel the hardness of my cock against her.

"What are we doing Alex?" Her tone is timid yet determined.

Firmly gripping her thighs, "I was getting ready to devour my new favorite meal in this kitchen."

"No," her voice firmer, "I'm being serious. What are we doing?"

Fuck.

Her telling me, 'no,' only makes me need her more.

I don't think that's a word a woman has ever said to me.

At least not when she was nearly naked with my hard cock pressed against her.

"*Cerecita,*" her name growls from my chest as I unbutton my shirt, "Are you denying me what I so desperately need?"

She watches my fingers work the buttons of my shirt, her chest heaving more with each one undone.

"I am being serious," I toss my shirt to the floor and begin to undo my belt, "I'm going to eat that sweet little pussy of yours until you're begging me to stop.

"Then, I'm going to climb onto this counter and pin you to it," I slowly pull my belt from my pants, "and I'm going to shove my bare cock into your tight little cunt."

Her eyes widen at the thought of me fucking her bare, but she doesn't even attempt to argue.

"Feeling all of you, I'm going to fuck you slow and hard," my fingers work the button and zipper of my pants, "Savoring you. Fucking you until you're screaming my name and my cock is the only one you remember."

Her breasts tremble with every stuttered breath she takes, and her eyes are filled with need.

She is incapable of denying me.

Her body craves me as much as I crave hers.

"Fucking you bare," I repeat my unbridled desire to take her without protection, "I'm going to empty every last drop of me inside of you when I come."

Lowering my pants and freeing my throbbing cock, I watch as she desperately chews at her lower lip.

"My dirty little girl likes the thought of being pumped full of my cum," I kick my pants off toward the other clothes on the floor, "Doesn't she?"

"Yes," she groans as her hips rock needily on the counter, frantically searching for relief.

Gripping my cock, I slowly stroke it as I stand before her. Her eyes focus on the slow pumps of my fist, and I watch as she swallows hard while listening to my words.

"And once you're so full of my cum that it's dripping from you," I rub the fat head of my cock along her slit over her panties, "I'm going to take you out.

"You're going to be on my arm," I grip her panties tightly with both hands, "proudly letting my cum slowly drip down your thighs. Not giving a fuck who sees.

"Thinking about how fucking eager you are," a loud, breathy moan bellows from her as I tear the panties from her body, "for me to fill you up again.

"Fuck, *cerecita*. Look how fucking wet you are," my finger drags through her slit, "just thinking about my bare cock pumping you full of my cum."

She whimpers as my finger rubs over her clit, her hips pressing her against my hand.

"Do you still want me to wait?" I slide my finger inside her slick cunt with ease, "Or does my dirty little girl want me to give her everything I know she desires?"

"Please," her hips rock, trying to take in more of my finger.

"Tell me," Her back arches as my finger curls inside of her.

"Please fuck me," she begs breathlessly.

"Until what?" My finger continues to work her, bringing her to the edge.

"Until I forget everyone else," her words tremble from her lips, "and I'm full of your cum."

"That's a good little girl," I growl, dropping to my knees and pressing my face firmly between her thighs.

My tongue on her clit and finger continuing to curl inside of her, it only takes a second to push her over the edge. Gripping my hair, her heels digging into my back, she rides my tongue through her much-needed release.

A man of my word, I continue lapping mercilessly at her pussy. Her arousal coating my face as she repeatedly comes undone until she is writhing on the counter and begging for me to stop.

thirteen

ISABELLA

Laying on the counter, Alex makes good on his promises.

Fuck, does he ever make good on them.

My hands pinned above my head with one hand, and my hip with his other, Alex continues to fuck me into the cold marble of the counter. Repeatedly, he slowly pulls out and drives into me hard. His massive cock rubbing against every sensitive nerve with each thrust.

"That's it, *cerecita*," his lips pepper kisses down my neck, "I was the first man to make you come, and I intend to be the last."

Wait...

What?

My thoughts are immediately interrupted by the orgasm that trembles through my body.

"Come all over my cock," he growls against my skin as he picks up the speed of his hips.

I don't even have a chance to come down from my euphoria as his deep, hard thrusts quickly have me on the edge of another.

"Fuck, Alex!" My legs wrap tightly around his waist as I come again.

His tongue plunges into my open mouth, muffling the screams of my release. My screams mix with his groans. As our tongues and feral noises blend together, I feel his hips tremble against me and his cock throbbing as he unleashes his streams of cum inside of me.

Releasing the grip he held on my wrists, Alex's hand begins to stroke the sweaty hair from my face.

"You're so fucking perfect, Isabella," his lips press against my forehead as he pulls himself from inside of me, "I can't fucking get enough of you."

"Alex?" I struggle to push out his name as he settles on his side next to me on the counter.

Laying next to me, one hand propping up his head and the other slowly tracing the curves of my body, he stares at me as though I am the most amazing being he has ever laid eyes on.

No one has ever looked at me with the adoration of this man.

"What did you say?" I nearly mumble the words.

"That you're fucking perfect," he repeats himself, "and I can't get enough of you."

"No...I...I mean," I stammer, "during."

"I'm going to need you to be a little more specific," he smirks down at me as his fingers run along my jaw.

"About being the first," I hesitate, "and last."

"That," he continues to smirk at me, "I think it was pretty straight-forward."

"Alex," I blurt out his name as though I'm scolding him, sitting up so quickly I nearly fall from the counter.

Rolling onto his back, his fingers lace behind his head as he gets comfortable. He looks like his ever calm and collected self, and I must look like a raging loon.

"It's been two days," I adjust myself on the counter so that I am facing him, "You barely know me. Are you serious?"

He doesn't say a word. He just lays there silently, like a man who confessed nothing more than loving pineapple on his pizza.

Oh my God! I hardly know anything about this man.

What if he does actually love pineapple on his pizza?

I physically shudder at the thought.

Needing a moment, I slide myself from the counter. I didn't hear him move, but I don't make it far before Alex has his arms wrapped around me and is pressed against my back.

"You don't build an empire and become a man as successful as me," he holds me firmly but comfortingly, "by making rash decisions."

Spinning in his arms, I look up at him, "Seriously? You don't think this is a rash decision?"

"I have never been more sure of a decision in my entire life," his fingers slide under my chin, "Two hours after we met, I knew you were unlike any woman I have ever met in my life."

"Alex..." His name a slow, mere whisper that sounds like it is going to be followed by tears.

"After two days with you, I know with certainty that I am not willing to let you go."

My heart is pounding in my chest as he continues to stare into my eyes as he speaks.

"I meant what I said," his lips press against mine, "But I want to give you a whole lifetime of firsts and lasts."

"Alex..." His name the only word I seem to be able to say at the moment, but he waits quietly for me to gather my thoughts.

"This is crazy," I stare up at him, "We barely know each other."

"I know everything I need to, and I'll spend my life learning the rest," his eyes are locked on mine, "And you might think this is crazy, but you haven't said, 'no.'"

He's right.

I don't even know if I want to reject his proposal.

It's crazy. Fucking insane even.

Who says yes to marrying someone they just met?

People in Vegas all the fucking time, Izzy.

"Yes," the single word comes from my mouth, surprising even myself, "This is fucking insane, but I'll marry you."

fourteen

ALEJANDRO

Izzy has been making herself at home in the steam shower for at least the last thirty minutes. Her timing couldn't have been more perfect. It allowed Andres to drop off the gift I ordered for her from Bergdorf's, without her knowing. It also gave me the opportunity to finish up making my plans for the two of us this evening in private.

Placing the large box on the bed, I head into the bathroom to join Izzy in the shower.

"You can't stay in here forever," I chuckle, startling her when I open the shower door.

"Try and stop me," she smiles back at me.

"Don't tempt me. I will happily keep you locked up in this apartment for the foreseeable future," I stalk toward her and box her body against the wall, "but then you won't have much need for the box I just left on the bed."

"I haven't been in here that long," she dips under my extended arm, "how in the world did you have time to go and get me anything?"

"I have my ways," I turn off the water and wrap her in a towel, before grabbing one for myself.

Following her into the bedroom, I love the squeal she makes when she sees the massive white box wrapped in a black satin bow. I lay on the bed beside the box, watching her delicately pull the bow to untie it. Carefully opening the box, her eyes are sparkling with excitement as she takes in the contents.

"Alex," she begins pulling the items from the box. A short, embellished black dress from Versace, a pair of Jimmy Choo stilettos, and a matching bra and crotchless panty set from La Perla's Black Label.

Holding the small amount of fabric comprising the crotchless panties in the air, she raises a questioning eyebrow at me.

"I think I was pretty clear," I sit up on the bed and pull her into my lap, "I want my cum dripping down your thighs, *cerecita*. And I don't want anything getting in the way if I decide I want to play with that sweet little cunt of mine while we are out this evening."

Watching for her reaction, she swallows hard.

"Tell me," I stand her from my lap, "Does the idea of me fucking you in public scare you or excite you?"

"Both," her cheeks redden as she answers me.

"Good. Now go get ready," my palm gently taps her ass, "and I'll help you get dressed when you're done."

Once she is back in the bathroom and I hear the blow dryer, I grab my phone from the nightstand.

> Everything ready for this evening?

ANDRES

Yes

> No problems?

One, but I took care of it

> And the other matter?

All set for tomorrow.

I'll let you know ASAP if anything comes up

Heading into the closet, I grab a black Tom Ford suit, a dark gray button-down shirt, and a pair of Oxfords. By the time I have dressed, a stunningly naked Izzy is walking from the bathroom. Her hair and make-up are impeccably done, both only accentuating how naturally beautiful she is.

Walking to the box, she picks up the bra and panties.

"I said I would help you," I take the undergarments from her and kneel on the floor before her in my suit.

Placing the bra on my bed, I hold the panties by her feet, allowing her to place her toes through the strappy garment. My fingers run the length of her legs as I pull the panties up to her hips. Adjusting the straps into their correct positions, I place a gentle kiss just above her clit before I stand. My fingers roam her skin as I pull the straps of the bra up to her shoulders. Turning her around, I push her hair to the side to fasten it.

Pulling the dress from the box, I help her step into it. Slowly dragging the zipper up her back, I watch as her muscles react to my delicate touch. Once she is zipped, I place a wet kiss on the nape of her neck and pull her hair into place over her back.

"Fuck, Alex," her words unmistakably breathy from her arousal, "How is it possible that you dressing me is as much a turn on as you undressing me?"

"My hands on your skin," I kiss her bare shoulder, "You know what it will feel like when I remove these clothes from you later. That is if I decide to remove them."

Kneeling before her, I slip her shoes onto her feet and buckle the straps around her ankles, before standing to admire the beautiful perfection that is soon going to be my wife.

"You are fucking amazing, *cerecita*."

fifteen

ISABELLA

"Where are you taking me?" I plead from the passenger seat as we drive.

I feel he got me quite dressed up to be cruising dark alleyways.

"You're going to need to be patient," his hand slides along my thigh. Between the crotchless panties and how short this dress is, he is easily able to brush his fingers against my pussy. And he does. Just enough to tease me.

"I need to make a quick stop to help Andres with something," he pulls the car to a stop in the middle of the alley.

"Here?" I look around at the questionable area we are in.

"It'll only be a minute," he exits the car and walks around to my door before helping me from the car.

He leads me to a door on his side of the car. Knocking twice, it opens and Andres is waiting on the other side. Alex passes him the keys to his Alfa Romeo, and Andres walks past us into the alley. As the door clicks shut, Alex places his hand on the small of my back, leading me down a dark hallway.

We turn a corner, and he walks me through the dark. Coming to a stop, he wraps his hand around my waist and the lights flicker on.

"I want the whole city to know you're going to be my wife," he pulls me tight against him, as I take in the view before me. It is a jewelry store, a luxurious, high-end jewelry store. It is well after hours, and they are open solely for us.

"Pick whatever one you want," he whispers against my ear, "I want you to love it, because you'll be wearing it for the rest of your life."

"Alex..." He ignores my discomfort at this situation and drags me to a display case and points to an absolutely gorgeous ring.

"I will not take no for an answer. I will worship you and spoil you as I see fit," leaning into my ear, he whispers quietly, "and that does not pertain to just the sweet little cunt you keep between your thighs."

Spending his money feels weird, even if I have agreed to be his wife.

"You'll get used to it," he speaks as though he reads my mind.

With him slowly walking behind me, I browse the contents of the display cases. Every single ring I pass is absolutely beautiful. Even the ones that aren't my style are stunning.

Like I have a style.

I walk past a ring that stops me in my tracks. Pointing at it in the display case, I look at the gentleman standing behind it and ask, "How much is this one?"

Turning, I see Alex shaking his head at the salesman.

"The One, in a 1.25 carat cushion cut diamond," he pulls the ring from the display, "is a Harry Winston favorite, ma'am."

My head snaps around to Alex.

Fucking Harry Winston?

In a matter of a few hours, you pulled a private shopping experience at Harry Fucking Winston?

Who are you?

"Would you like to try it on?" the salesman questions.

"Yes," Alex answers for me when I don't respond, "she would."

Taking the ring, Alex gently slides it on my finger.

"This is too much," I shake my head at the ring. It is gorgeous, more than most little girls dream about.

"Look at me," his finger under my chin tilts my face up to meet his. He stares at me for a moment in silence.

"This is the one," he says to the salesclerk without breaking eye contact with me, "We'll take it, and the coordinating wedding band as well. Would you like anything else, *cerecita*?"

I shake my head in response to his question. Without waiting for a total, he pulls his wallet from his jacket pocket and slides a credit card across the counter. A moment later, he is passed a receipt and a small bag containing the box for the wedding band.

"Thank you, Mr. Marcano," an elderly gentleman at the front of the door unlocks the door, "Please do not hesitate to reach out if you and Miss Drake would like to come shopping in privacy again."

"Thank you, Phillip," I watch as they shake hands, "We appreciate it."

Phillip opens the door for the two of us, and Alex walks me to the car Andres moved around to the front of the building.

"Ma'am," Andres nods his head at me as he passes the keys back to Alex, "You made a beautiful choice."

Alex hands the small bag to Andres, "I'd appreciate it if you could take this back to the penthouse."

"Of course, sir," he takes the bag and promptly gets into a Maserati parked behind the Alfa Romeo.

"Next time," his lips trail along the side of my neck, "I would appreciate it if you don't hesitate to let me spoil you. I plan to give you everything you didn't know you wanted from this life."

His teeth sink into the flesh at the base of my neck, and I yelp at the foreign pain of the sensation. Even as I hiss slightly through the little bit of pain it causes, I can feel the effect it has between my legs.

"Don't worry," his teeth trail along my ear, "I plan to spoil your cunt too."

sixteen

ALEJANDRO

All eyes were on Isabella throughout our dinner, the city gossips quickly trying to determine who this unknown girl on the arm of one of the city's most eligible bachelors is. The chatter only growing louder as people made note of the large ring on her finger, and the fact that I couldn't keep my eyes off her.

If only these people had any idea who I really was.

Leaving the restaurant, I motion for the valet to hand Izzy the keys. With all eyes on us at dinner, I couldn't touch her near the way I wanted to.

"I can't drive your car," she mutters back at me.

"Your car too," my hands discreetly roam her ass as I help her into the car.

Climbing into the passenger seat, my hand reaches for her thigh as she starts the ignition. Rubbing my fingers against her bare pussy, both Izzy and the car purr as she slips it into gear.

"Next time you wear panties like these," I growl with need, "we're going to have to go somewhere more discreet. I've been dying to tease you all night."

She groans and the car jerks forward when my finger taps against her clit.

"Pay attention to the road," my hands spread her thighs to make more room for me to play with her. She eagerly presses her left leg against the car door.

"Open your mouth for me," she does as I ask, and I slide my middle and ring finger over her tongue. Her lips close around my fingers, and she sucks on them while caressing them with her tongue. A moan rattles from my chest when I imagine her sucking my cock with those perfect pink lips wrapped around it.

She smirks as I pull my saliva coated fingers from her mouth.

She knows exactly what she's doing to me.

Sliding them through her slit, I press my fingers into her cunt. Curling them softly as the palm of my hand presses against her clit, I watch her hands grip the steering wheel.

Her breathy moans have an undeniable effect on me, and I use my free hand to adjust the growing cock in my pants.

"I'm not going to make it back to the apartment, *cerecita*," I continue to work my fingers in her slick cunt while palming my cock through my pants, "I need to be inside of you."

Picking up the speed of my fingers inside of her, I rub my palm against her clit. Her hips grind back against me, and the breathy squeals coming from her telling me how close she is to coming.

Watching her writhe in pleasure only increases my need.

Pulling into the parking garage, she quickly finds my space and pulls into it. The moment she puts it in park, I undo her seatbelt. With my fingers still inside of her, I pull her over the console and onto my lap.

"We made it," she grunts, riding my lap as my fingers work her fast and hard.

"Not even close," I wrap my arm around her waist and grind my cock against her ass, "The moment you come for me, I'm tearing this fucking dress from you and filling you with my cum again."

Her head falls back onto my shoulder, and she clenches around my fingers. The mere thought of me breeding her, throwing her over the edge, she cries out my name as she comes.

Pulling myself from her, I lean her forward and undo the zipper of her dress. My hands grip the fabric firmly at the base of the open zipper and I tear it at the seam. Before leaning her back against me, I hastily undo my pants and free my cock. Lifting her slightly, I align myself with her entrance and pull her over my length eliciting a groan from us both.

The two of us pull the remnants of her dress from her and toss it into the driver's seat. Sitting between my legs, my hand snakes around her neck as I hold her back to my chest. Her hips rock, grinding her over my length.

"Fuck," I groan into her neck, "That's it. Grind that ass against me and ride my big fucking cock."

Izzy's hips continue to roll on my lap, our rapid breaths quickly fogging over the windows of the car. My hips flex to meet hers, needing to be deeper inside of her.

"Be a good girl," my free hand presses between her thighs and rubs on her clit, "and come all over my lap."

Her hips move faster on my thighs, grinding herself on my cock and my hands, chasing her climax.

"That's it," I whisper against her ear, "Come for me like a good little girl.

I slowly begin to increase the speed and pressure of my fingers on her clit, "because once you do, I'm going to spread you across the hood of this car and fuck you like the dirty little girl you really are."

"Some...one...will...see," her hips work hard against me.

"You're mine, *cerecita*. No man would dare be stupid enough to look at you," I bite down on her neck and suck hard enough to mark her.

seventeen

ISABELLA

As Alex sucks on my neck and drives his cock up into me, I lose control. Gripping the headrest behind him, I grind down on him hard as every muscle in body spasms against him.

"Such a good fucking girl," he growls against my neck while pushing the car door open.

With his cock still buried inside of me, he slides the two of us from the car. I attempt to cover myself but notice the two men usually at guard outside the elevator are standing facing the wall with their backs turned to us.

"I'd take their fucking eyes for even thinking about looking at you."

Fuck. That's dark.

He roughly drops me, stomach first onto the hood of the car and slams his cock into me. His hands on my back, he pushes me onto the hard metal of the car as he relentlessly pounds into me. Every thrust, painfully slamming my hips against the side of the car, causing me to cry out in both pleasure and pain.

I feel his hand undo the clasp of my bra before his hands work their way between my body and the car. Firmly gripping both of my breasts, he lifts me toward him, continuing to hammer me against the fender of the car.

The new angle repeatedly slides him over the spot that undoes me, but he doesn't let me come. Instead, he brings me to the edge before pulling himself from me.

"I want to watch those big, beautiful tits bounce as I drive into you," he lays me back on the hood and rolls me over and grabs my thighs. Shoving his length back into me, he savagely drives himself into me. His grip on me, the only thing keeping me from inching across the hood with every thrust.

"I want you to watch how well your tight little cunt takes my cock," his arms wrap tighter around my thighs, and he pulls them further apart to provide me a better view of where our bodies meet, "How it quivers and squeezes around me when you come."

"Alex!" My hands claw at his hands around my thighs as I come painfully hard.

"And..how...fucking...needy...it...is...," he grunts through his thrusts as my thighs shake violently in his hold, "to be filled...with my...fucking cum."

He lets out an animalist roar, his hips stuttering against me as his cock throbs through his release inside of me.

Continuing to slowly work his cock in and out of me, both of us trembling from the sensitivity of the sensation, he releases the bruising grip he held on my thighs. Pulling his softening cock from me, he helps me sit on the edge of the hood.

He tucks himself into his pants and removes his jacket. Lifting me from the car, he places my feet on the ground and pulls the jacket around my shoulders. Sliding my arms into the oversized jacket, I pull it around me to cover myself as he retrieves my purse from the car.

"Boys," I acknowledge the two men averting their gaze from me as we enter the elevator.

I could strut naked in front of them, and they wouldn't look.

Is Alex really that scary of a boss?

His arms wrap around me from behind as the elevator doors close, and his lips are immediately nuzzling into the crook of my neck. "You should call your parents, *cerecita*. Tell them the news."

My dad is going to lose his shit...

Digging my phone from my purse, I hold out my hand with the engagement ring and take a picture.

I have exciting news...

MOM

What Izz? Did you find a new job?

Not quite

I text her the photo of the ring.

The phone rings as we are stepping off the elevator. Relieved it's not FaceTime with my current appearance, I answer, "Hi Mom. You're on speaker."

"Isabella Drake," her mom tone bellows through the phone, "Please tell me you aren't marrying that cheating piece of shit. Ian, you don't deserve her, especially not after how you've treated her. And you had the nerve to propose with a fake ring?"

"Mom...Mom," I watch Alex snicker at her comments as I try to interrupt her rant to get her attention, "Mom! I'm not marrying Ian."

"Thank fucking God," she mumbles.

The phone is silent for a second before her voice comes through the other end again, "Wait? Who the hell are you marrying?"

"Hello, Mrs. Drake," Alex's voice is smooth and sultry, "I'm Alejandro Marcano...Alex...and I truly wish I could be introducing myself to you in person. I would love it if you and Mr. Drake could join us for dinner tomorrow night. We can come to you in Fairfield if that is easier."

"No," she sounds unsure, "We can come to your place, Izzy."

"I'll text you the address."

"I know where you live, Isabella."

"Mom," I'm going to freak her out, "I'm staying at Alex's place. We'll see you and Dad tomorrow?"

"Y...yes," she answers.

"Love you. Bye, Mom."

"Love you, dear."

She must think I can't hear her or that she hangs up, because I hear her nervously call for my dad, "George..."

Before I forget, I drop her a few texts.

> 355 East 72nd Street
>
> And warn Dad...
>
> Alex is a little older

eighteen

ALEJANDRO

The sun won't start to rise for a few hours, as I stand over Izzy. Laying on her stomach, her red hair is splayed across the black silk sheets. The smooth, porcelain skin on her back is fully exposed.

Even in her sleep, she is fucking perfection.

Leaving a note and my credit card on her nightstand, I pull the sheet up to her shoulders and gently kiss her temple.

Quietly, I close the bedroom door and walk to the end of hall and enter the passcode on the locked door. Stepping inside, the sensors cause the lights to flicker on. Grabbing two 9mm Lugers, I tuck them into my waistband at the back of my pants before putting two extra magazines in the pocket of my jacket.

Stepping from the mini armory, I pull the door shut as quietly as possible. I give the handle a jiggle to ensure it's locked, and head down to the garage to meet Andres and Eduardo.

Both of my men are waiting for me in the garage when the elevator doors open. Walking to the far side of the garage, Andres pops the trunk to a late-model, black, BMW. He grabs masks for the three of us. Climbing into the car, I take a seat in the rear.

I can't fight off an attack I don't see coming. I won't make the same mistakes my father made.

"We should be to the shipyard in about thirty minutes," Andres informs me from behind the steering wheel.

"And the boat?" I question.

"Arriving in an hour," Eduardo responds, "According to our guy in customs, several guys from the Cardenas family are already waiting for the container."

"Good," I nearly hear Andres smile in anticipation at my response.

Maybe a fucking blood bath will teach them to keep their shit out of my fucking city.

I pull my mask over my head as we approach the security gates.

You don't run the largest international drug cartel in secret if everyone knows what your face looks like.

Two men who work for my cartel have seen my face – Andres and Eduardo. The rest have only ever seen me covered in a black ski mask with mesh to cover my eyes and a skeleton printed across the face. Most have also never seen Andres or Eduardo's faces either.

At eighteen, I killed the man who murdered my family, and resumed my birthright – The Diaz Cartel. Taking my mother's name, I immigrated to the United States and became a true American success story. A poor immigrant to New York City's most eligible billionaire bachelor. Alejandro Marcano, ruthless CEO of the world's most successful import and export corporation.

Not my fault no one suspects the world's largest legitimate import and export business is also the world's largest narcotics supplier.

"Up here," I tap Andres's shoulder, "On the right. We'll walk the rest of the way."

Pulling on my gloves, the three of us climb from the car and walk toward the boat dock where the Cardena's shipping container will be unloaded. There are four men waiting, needing to unload their shipment before Customs has an opportunity to search it.

Andres pulls his knife from the holster on his waistband, as Eduardo and I both pull our guns.

Silently stalking toward the unsuspecting men, we are within feet of them before they notice we are coming. Raising my arms, I fire both pistols, shooting a bullet into the torso of two of the men. Eduardo fires his gun at the back of the third man's head, killing him instantly. The fourth man never sees Andres coming when he slashes his neck from behind.

Standing over one of the two men I shot, I fire again. This bullet goes through the center of his forehead. It is immediately echoed by Eduardo finishing the other guy.

Walking to the man with the slit throat, he is still struggling for his last breath as he drowns in his own blood. A gurgled groan bubbles from his throat when I shove my gloved finger into his wound. Sliding my finger across his forehead, I ensure the Cardenas cartel knows exactly who was responsible for the death of their men.

"It's a good fucking thing your last name wasn't Hernandez," Andres jokes when he looks down at the man he killed and my handywork.

"Funny," I deadpan, "You should go on tour with that comedic act of yours."

The three of us make our way back to the car, ensuring that we aren't seen. We will be long gone by the time the police arrive. And when they find this car, it'll be an inferno in Bushwick.

No face.

No identity.

Untraceable.

Leaving the shipyard, I pull my mask and gloves off, tossing them onto the seat beside me.

Andres drops me a few blocks from my office, and I walk the rest of the way, stopping for a coffee on my way. My car has been parked in the garage for about an hour, the GPS providing me with an alibi in the event it is needed in the future.

Sipping my coffee in the elevator, I look at my watch.

My cerecita should be waking up any moment now.

nineteen

ISABELLA

The alarm clock blaring on my phone wakes me.

What the fuck...

I didn't set an alarm.

Groggily flailing my arm at the bedside table to find my phone, I sigh when I can't locate it. I realize that I am alone in the bed when I open my eyes and sit up. My phone has been moved to the far side of the nightstand. Sitting on top of my buzzing phone is a navy-blue envelope.

Grabbing the envelope and my phone, I silence the alarm before sitting against the headboard. Opening the envelope, a black credit card falls from it when I pull out the notecard.

CERECITA—

I HATED LEAVING YOU THIS MORNING, BUT
I HAD TO GET TO THE OFFICE FOR AN EARLY
MEETING. I'M GOING TO BE TIED UP ALL DAY.
GO SPOIL YOURSELF. I EXPECT YOU TO FILL
YOUR SIDE OF THE CLOSET AND BUY PLENTY OF
LINGERIE FOR ME TO TEAR FROM YOUR BODY.
THE GUYS DOWNSTAIRS KNOW WHERE TO TAKE
YOU. I'LL BE HOME IN TIME FOR DINNER.
ALL MY LOVE, ALEX

Just as I am about to put the phone back on the bedside table and place my head back on the pillow, it buzzes in my lap.

ALEX

You don't have all day cerecita

Time to get up

I am...

So you weren't just laying back down?

My eyes dart around the room.

How the hell did he know that?

I have twenty minutes before my next meeting

> Just enough time for you to try
> something new

> And what is that?

> Sit up against the headboard and pull
> your knees up to your chest

> Why?

> Headboard. Knees to chest.

Hesitating for a moment, I do as he says, waiting for the next text to come through.

> Put one of my pillows at your feet

> Lean the phone against it, so you can
> see my texts

Setting the phone down, I'm about to rest my back against the headboard when another comes through.

> Answer the phone

His text no more than comes through and a FaceTime call from Alex pops up on my phone. Pushing the button, I answer the call and smile at seeing his face.

"Good morning beautiful," he smiles back at me, "Lose the sheet and let me see you."

Slowly, I begin to pull back the sheet and he growls through the call, "Fuck. I should've woken you before I left. Spread those feet and let me see that beautiful pussy of yours. Don't be shy. You know if I was there, I'd have my face buried in it right now."

Spreading my feet apart, I feel so vulnerable. I feel as though I am on display for him.

"Touch my pussy for me, *cerecita*."

Hesitantly, I bring my hand between my legs.

He knows I've never done this before.

"Don't think about it," his voice is powerfully encouraging, "Close your eyes. Use your fingers to part your lips and spread yourself open for me."

Following his directions, he showers me with praise, "Good girl. That sweet, sweet cunt. Always so fucking wet and ready for me."

I can feel the neediness growing beneath my hand as my chest starts to rise and fall at a quicker pace.

"Keep your eyes closed. Pretend that's my hand," his voice is a deep, gravelly whisper, "Put it where you want to be touched."

Placing my fingers on my clit, a tiny whimper leaves my mouth.

"Now move them the way you want me to touch you," he pauses as I glide them over my clit. Rubbing and massaging it slowly, my hips begin rocking against my hand.

I groan from my own touch between my legs.

"I fucking love watching you play with your pussy," Alex groans, "Are you thinking about my fingers or my tongue rubbing over your cunt?"

"Neither," I struggle to push out the word.

"Are you thinking about my cock?"

"Mm-hmm," my fingers work faster.

"It's so fucking hard for you right now. Are you thinking about it stretching you?" He pauses for a moment as I work myself closer to the edge, "Or filling you with cum?"

"Both..."

"Come for me like a good little girl," he growls, "and I'll give you everything you're fantasizing about tonight."

"Please...Alex...Yes!" The words tremble from my mouth as I make myself come.

Opening my eyes as I come down, Alex has ended the call. I'm still panting when I pick up the phone.

> Always such a good little girl for me
>
> I look forward to rewarding you later
>
> Go clean up
>
> Then go buy something for me to reward you in

twenty

ISABELLA

I take a quick selfie in the mirror of the lacy, black teddy and high heels I have on, and text it to Alex before changing back into my own clothes. Regardless of what the guy driving me around has to say, this is going to be my last store.

I am exhausted, and I really want to take a shower before my parents arrive.

Every store the driver took me to today was outlandishly expensive, and I feel like I have spent way too much of Alex's money. If it weren't for the occasional text praising me for spoiling myself and more promises of him spoiling me later, I probably would've stopped hours ago.

ALEX

Fuck cerecita

You know I'm in a meeting

I'm sorry I interrupted

You never interrupt!

But now all I can think about is tearing that off you

Wear that for me tonight.

And buy two, because you won't be wearing that one again

Looking at the price tag, I swallow hard.

One thousand and ninety-five dollars.

He's crazy.

Fuck...you might not make it through dinner

Alex! My parents are going to be there!

I'll see my dirty little girl soon

Certifiable even.

Knowing I won't have time to put all these clothes away, I shove it in the back of the closet when I get back to the penthouse. I take a quick shower, my hair pulled up so I don't have to wash it. As I'm drying off, I hear my phone ding.

MOM

Sweetheart we're going to be early

Dad insisted we leave early but we
made great time on the Cross Bronx

We'll be there in 30 minutes

*Fuck, Alex isn't supposed to be home for another hour. I
don't think I can take this inquisition on my own.*

OK see you soon.

I pull up my favorites and call Alex. No answer.

ALEX

Still in a meeting dirty little girl

Can you leave early?

Ending my meeting and leaving now

You don't want to know why?

You need me

That's the only reason I need

Be there as quickly as I can

*How in the hell did I manage to land the world's most
perfect man?*

*Rich...considerate...drop everything for me...a gentleman...
except when he's not...fucks like a God...Is there anything
wrong with him?*

I drop my phone onto the vanity, quickly apply my make-up and spruce up the curls in my hair before heading into the closet. After walking to the huge pile of bags, I dig through the La Perla bag to find the teddy Alex intends to destroy this evening. After considering all of the clothes I bought today, I settle on what's in the bag from Bergdorf's. The dark denim, midi, wrap dress will be perfect for what I have in mind. Pulling it on over the teddy, I secure the two buckles on the hip and slip on the black strappy heels the salesgirl recommended to go with it. Walking into the bedroom, I take a glance in the mirror before grabbing my phone and heading downstairs.

That'll do.

My phone buzzes in my hand as I reach the bottom of the stairs.

MOM

We're in the lobby, are you sure you gave us the right address?

Yes.

Tell the front desk your name

They're expecting you and they'll let you up

A few minutes later the elevator doors ding, and I hear my mom hesitantly call out, "Izz?"

"You're in the right place, Mom."

As they walk further into the penthouse, I wonder if I made the same awestruck face the first time I saw this place too.

"Alex isn't home yet," I hug my mom and then my dad, "but he's on his way and should be here any minute."

"You look wonderful Izzy," my mom's eyes continue to roam as she walks toward the windows, "The skyline view from up here is absolutely amazing."

"That's why I bought the place," Alex dons his ever-charming smile from the elevator as he quickly closes the distance between us.

"You must be Alex's father," Dad's words slow as Alex slides his hand around my hip.

Squeezing my waist gently, Alex leans down and places a light kiss just below my ear, "You look incredible, *cerecita. Lo suficientemente buena para comer.*"

Ugh...here we go.

"Mom, Dad," I grab the hand on my hip, "This is Alex."

"A pleasure to finally meet you, George," Alex takes my awestruck father's hand and shakes it before turning to my mom, "And you as well, Julie. I have heard so much about you both."

"I feel like we can't say the same about you," Dad uses the fatherly tone I was dreading.

"George," my mom scolds him.

"I'm sure the two of you have a lot of questions," Alex gestures toward the living room and removes his jacket.

"Yeah," Dad mumbles, "Like how old you are."

"Dad!"

"What?" he replies, "It's a fair question."

I take a seat next to Alex on the loveseat and watch Mom pull Dad down next to her on the couch. I'm pretty sure she mumbles, "Behave."

twenty one

ALEJANDRO

"Forty-two, George," I respond, my tone firm but noncombative, "And now you're also wondering why someone my age is with Isabella. And am I just some rich guy taking advantage of your little girl?"

George doesn't answer, but the look on his face speaks volumes.

"We just have some, um...concerns," Julie looks between me and Isabella. "I can get over the age difference. Hell, I dated a guy twenty years older than me before I married your father."

"You what?" George sits up straight and stares at his wife, leaving me fighting the urge to laugh out loud.

"You know about James," she responds to him and returns her attention to the two of us. "You only broke up with Ian a couple of weeks ago. I'm happy you aren't sitting around moping over him, but why the rush for the two of you to get married. You obviously just met."

"Dad has told me since I was little that he knew on your first date that he was going to marry you," Isabella looks back at her mom. Squeezing my hand she turns her attention to me, "I know it's crazy. We both do. But we know."

Over dinner, a few drinks, and several hours of heartfelt conversation, I think I can safely say that George no longer wants to murder me. I can't quite say he's excited to have me as a son-in-law, but reluctantly agreeing to a few months' long engagement seemed to at least be making a step in the right direction.

"Next weekend," Julie hugs me goodbye, "You'll come to our place for dinner?"

George firmly shakes my hand before hugging Isabella goodbye. His words a mixture of sincerity and being in jest, "Are you sure you aren't pregnant?"

"Jesus, Dad," she jokingly shoves him into the elevator, "Bye."

"Not yet anyway," I smirk, whispering into her ear just as the elevator doors close. Ignoring my comment, she begins walking back into the living room.

"That went better than I thought," she walks to the windows before turning back to face me.

"I'm rich and charming," I smile back at her as she fidgets with the buckle on her dress, "And I make you happy. Of course, they'd like me."

"And to think," she pulls the buckle on her dress, and it draws open down the front before she drops it to the ground, "I just like you for your huge cock."

"Fuck, *cerecita*," my cock grows uncomfortably confined in my pants at the sight of her. The dress pooled around her tall black heels, her thick thighs, and that tiny, lacy, black teddy barely containing her curves.

"I'm pretty sure you said something about fulfilling my fantasies and tearing this off me," she smirks at me, before turning and strutting her beautiful ass closer to the floor-to-ceiling windows.

"First," I untuck my shirt and begin slowly undoing the buttons of my shirt, "Spread those legs for me. Show me how you touch your pussy and get it nice and wet for me."

Without hesitation, she widens her stance and slides her fingers underneath the lace. Removing my shirt as I walk toward her, I can see her fingers working through the sheer fabric. Reaching her, I undo my belt and pull it from my pants before dropping it to the floor.

"Are you thinking about my cock again?" I palm the throbbing bulge in my pants as I stand inches from her.

"Yes," she moans.

"And how it's going to stretch out your cunt?" My free hand rubs against the lace over her hand rubbing her clit.

"No," her hips grind against her hand.

"Tell me," I demand, gripping her jaw and pulling her face up to mine.

"How...you'd...feel," her words slow and breathy, "sliding...over...my tongue."

"Rub your clit, *cerecita*. Bring yourself to the edge," I tilt her face to my hand stroking my cock through my pants, "But don't come, and I'll let you suck my cock."

Her hips grind harder against her hand, with a neediness I have yet to see from her, "I'll let you swallow every inch of me down your throat."

"Please," she strokes me with her free hand while diligently working over her clit with the other. Her eye lids are heavy and her lower lip trembles as she sits on the brink.

Undoing my pants, I pull my cock from my boxers and slowly stroke it to further taunt her. Her eyes focused on my cock, her hips quiver against her hand and her teeth bite painfully hard at her lower lip as she struggles not to come.

"You're doing such a good job," I praise her, watching as tears well in the corner of her eyes as her mind fights so hard against what her body needs.

"Such a good little girl," my hand gently strokes the side of her face, "listening so well and only coming for me.

"Take what you've earned," I smile down her with pride, "and then I'll fuck the neediness from your cunt."

twenty two

ISABELLA

Previous men have made sucking cock feel like a chore, but not Alex. Alex makes me feel like I need to savor this gift that I've earned. Dropping to my knees, I wrap my hands around his shaft as I slowly lick him from balls to tip. The neediness between my thighs only growing.

He groans as I suck the head of his cock while he gathers my hair from my face. Fisting his base, I take more of him into my mouth. The lips of my already full mouth brush against my fist, and I realize how much more of him there is to take.

"You look so beautiful on your knees before me," he praises me.

Trying to take him deeper, I gag on the thickness of him. Unsuccessfully, I try again and tears well in my eyes as I audibly gag around him.

"It's okay if you can't take it all this time," his hand strokes the side of my face as my eyes stare up at him, "Your mouth feels so fucking good sliding over my cock, and we'll teach your throat to take it too."

I continue to swallow him to my fist as I stroke the base of his shaft. My hips flex as I suck him harder as deep as I can, as the neediness between my thighs begins to ache.

With his hand under my chin, Alex pulls himself from my mouth while helping me to my feet.

"You bowed before your king. Now let me bow to my queen," he drops to his knees before me. I watch as Alex's fingers press through the lace, and my body jerks as he shreds the delicate fabric providing him full access to me. The scraps of the lingerie left hanging from my body, his hands firmly grip my ass, and he pulls me onto his tongue. Fervently licking and sucking at my clit until the needy ache is gone and I'm struggling to stay on my feet.

"Hands on the glass," he holds my hips close to him, forcing me to bend at the waist. As my hands press flat against the cool pane of glass, Alex presses his tip against me. My whole body tingles, as though an electric current flows through me, when he slowly slides the length of him inside of me.

"Fuck," he groans, "I love watching your tight little cunt getting stretched by my cock."

He pulls out and slams back into me, causing me to cry out. His thrusts are relentless and punishing, willing me to come. Prying it from me.

Fisting my hair, he pulls my head, forcing me to arch my back. The new angle drags him along my walls, and I scream out his name as I come.

My screams only make him drive deeper and harder, until he is grunting into me with every savage blow. As I come again, my exhausted body presses against the glass. With the cold glass pressed against my face and chest, Alex's hot and sweaty body presses to my back as his thrusts become slower and deeper.

"I want to fill you with my cum," he growls against my neck, "but I can't get enough of fucking you. I can't get enough of you."

"Alex..." I feel myself tighten around him as I struggle through the pleasure of coming again.

"Fuuuuuck," he drives up into me hard one final time, his hips flexed holding him deep inside of me as he comes.

EIGHTEEN MONTHS LATER

"Alex," I feign struggling against his hold, "Really? Here?"

"Yes, *cerecita*," he yanks me back to him and wiggles my skirt over my hips.

"You can't argue about getting fucked in public," the palm of his hand comes down over my bare ass and I stifle my yelp, "when you come to dinner with no panties."

His hand strikes me again and I struggle not to cry out.

"This also isn't the first time I've fucked my wife in a public restroom. Just be happy I managed to pull you from the table."

Turning me around, he grips my thighs and hoists me around his waist as he drives my back into the door. His lips on my ear as he slides into me, "So fucking wet for someone who doesn't want to be fucked."

He knows me so fucking well.

"I missed this sweet fucking cunt while I was gone," he pulls nearly out of me and slides back in. "Three days is way too fucking long."

"I'm going to take you fast and hard," his hips work him in and out of me at a quick pace. The goal solely to come before we get caught. "I'll give you what I know you need."

He devilishly smirks at me as his hand clamps over my mouth and he drives me hard into the door. I bite his palm to hold back my screams, and he hisses against my neck. My legs flex around his waist, pulling him deeper into me as I come.

Pulling himself from me, he lowers my feet to the ground and fists himself, "Now clean your cream from my cock like a good little girl."

My skirt still scrunched around my waist, I kneel before him and take him in to the base. My lips and tongue working up and down his shaft, I suck the tangy taste of my arousal from him.

His fingers fist through my hair, prompting me to take him more vigorously.

"That's it," he groans as I continuously take him deep, "swallow my cock while I spill my cum down your throat."

His cock hardens in my mouth as I feel him pump his release into my throat.

Lifting me back to my feet, he tucks himself back into his pants and pulls my skirt back into place. He places a soft, wet kiss on my lips as he palms the sides of my face.

"God, I fucking missed you," he whispers as he pulls back from me.

twenty three

ALEJANDRO

Quickly silencing my alarm from ringing, hoping not to wake Isabella, I lay my phone back on the bedside table.

"Baby," she groans, rubbing her hand over my chest, "What time is it?"

Three in the morning.

"Early," I place my hand on top of hers on my chest, "I have to go deal with some things at the office this morning. Go back to sleep, *cerecita*."

My hand slowly stroking her arm, she is sleeping again within minutes. Lifting her hand, I kiss her palm, and lay it on the warmth of my pillow as I slide from the bed.

Pulling on jeans and a black hooded sweatshirt, I slip on my boots and head to the elevator. Going down a floor, I unlock the door to the apartment I rented when Isabella moved in with me. It is pretty much vacant, with the exception of a small kitchenette, table and the bedroom converted to an armory.

While she is my wife, the love of life, I still have not told her who I really am. It is not from fear that she will reject me. She loves me as unconditionally as I love her, and I know that she will accept me regardless of my flaws. I just don't want to tarnish the one clean and pure thing I have in my life by bringing her into this dark and dirty world.

Grabbing a short-barreled shotgun and a pistol, I lock the armory behind me and head downstairs to the garage.

ANDRES

Shipment arriving in 90 minutes

I'll be to the port in 45

I drive the Maserati to the office, where I park and promptly climb into the waiting Honda Civic with Eduardo. At this early hour, with the lack of city traffic, he gets us to the docks quickly.

All eyes turn to my masked face as I exit the car and walk toward the group of waiting men. In this mask, I am a man to be feared. Over the past twenty-five years, I have built my empire as a man who has no limits to protect what belongs to him. Ruthless. Brutal. Maybe even a tinge psychotic. That was all made abundantly clear the day I burned alive the men that dared to try to take my father's legacy from me.

"Boss," Andres's voice greets me from behind his mask.

"A," I nod back at him. Along with concealing our faces, I have a strict rule about anyone knowing my name or those of the two men I trust most with my life. As much as you can trust anyone in this world.

Turning my attention to the men standing with Andres, "When this shipment gets here, we have fifteen minutes to get it transferred to the cars and get out of here before the customs agents arrive."

They all stare back at me, knowing full well the punishment for disrespecting or failing me. "Split it between the cars and offload at the locations A provided you. Understood?"

Nods and a choir of, "Yes, boss" echo back at me.

In my gut, something feels off about today. I shift my gait and eye my surroundings carefully. While I don't see anything out of the ordinary, I can't shake this feeling that something about this shipment isn't right.

The metal shipping container is dropped on the dock and my men are immediately cutting the lock to gain access to my thousand kilos of cocaine. The moment the doors are open, they begin filing in to move the product to their awaiting cars.

"DEA," a voice bellows from behind me, "Freeze.".

Andres must see them first because he raises his gun around me and fires. Raising the shotgun, I don't have time to turn before I hear shots fired back in our direction. A searing pain stabs through my shoulder and knocks me off balance.

"Son of a fucking bitch," I grit through my teeth at the pain radiating through my shoulder and down my arm.

Spinning around, I squeeze the trigger to the shotgun and unload every shell into the men standing before me. Dropping it to the ground, I pull the Luger from the waistband of my pants. I try to take cover behind the door of the storage container while firing off shots.

My men are dropping to the ground nearly as fast as the DEA Agents.

Fuck.

Through the gun fight, I watch several of my vehicles flee the docks, getting my shipment out of here.

Heaven help the man who leads the DEA back to one of my warehouses.

Firing off a final shot, I kill the last of the agents, before collapsing to the ground.

"Boss," Andres grabs me under the arm and yanks me from my knees to my feet, "Fuck, boss."

His hand presses against my stomach, and I look down to realize I took two additional bullets in my flank. It's hard to notice, I'm dressed in only the black material, but my sweatshirt is saturated with my blood.

"We gotta get you to a hospital," Eduardo rushes to help Andres get me into the car.

"Fuck that," I groan through the pain, "take my phone. Call el doctor. Have him come to the apartment."

Sitting in the backseat with Andres's hands pressing against my wounds, gushing with every pump of my heart, things begin to grow hazy. Only small recollections of the drive are present.

Opening my eyes, I grunt as Andres and Eduardo drop me onto the small kitchenette table in my empty apartment.

This isn't fucking good...

The searing pain is fading, and keeping my eyes open is increasingly becoming a challenge.

"*Cerecita*," I groan, "Get Isabella."

"Boss?" Andres questions, knowing that she has not been made privy to this side of my life.

"Get her," I struggle to push out the words, "I won't die without saying goodbye to her."

twenty four

ISABELLA

The sun is just starting to shine through the bedroom windows, slowly waking me from my sleep. Stretching out my arm for Alex, I remember he said he had to leave early this morning. I hear a familiar voice yelling from the living room just as I was thinking about going back to sleep,

"Mrs. Marcano. Isabella?" I realize they sound panicked, "Ma'am? Alejandro needs you ma'am."

Andres?

What could Alex possibly need me for at this hour?

He isn't even here.

Sliding from bed, I grab my robe to cover myself and tie the belt quickly around my waist. Opening the bedroom door reveals Andres on the other side, which startles me.

"Ma'am," Andres reaches for my hand, "We have to go."

Looking down, I realize that his hand is covered in blood. Both of his hands are covered in blood. His arms and clothes are covered in it as well. It is only then that the nauseating, metallic smell hits me.

Nearly on autopilot, my body follows behind Andres. I feel numb, my brain unable to comprehend whatever it is that his happening in this moment.

"Andres," I stutter over the lump in my throat as he gently pulls me into the elevator, my bare feet stepping in puddles of cold, wet blood. "Whose blood is this?"

He doesn't answer. Dropping my hand, he pushes the button for the floor beneath ours and we ride in silence for the eternity it takes the elevator to travel the floor.

When the doors open, my body instinctively follows the trail of blood down the hallway.

So much blood.

Pushing open the door with the bloodied handprints, I step into a relatively dark, unfurnished apartment. Eduardo and a man I have never seen are hovering over a table, rash words coming from them both.

As I walk further into the apartment, I see more blood dripping from the table and pooling into the now stained carpet. When I realize who is laying on the table, my heart stops and stomach flops.

"Alex," the word whispers over my lips as I run to his side.

"Oh my God," I scream when I reach him.

He doesn't even look like my husband. His skin is grayish in appearance, his eyes sunken, and he looks frail and weak.

"What the hell are you doing?" I yell, my attention darting back to Andres and Eduardo, as I grab Alex's hand. "He needs to go to the fucking hospital."

"This is the hospital, señora," the man I've never seen speaks with a thick accent as he shoves an IV needle into Alex's arm.

"*Cerecita*," Alex's eyelids flutter and he squeezes my hand, "*lo siento.*"

"No!" I firmly squeeze his hand back with both of mine, "You don't get to be sorry."

"*Lo siento, mi amor,*" his words are so faint, they are nearly inaudible, "I have so much to tell you. So much you need to know."

"Don't you dare," tears trickle down my face when I realize why I was brought here.

Alex is going to die.

His grip on my hand loosens and I watch as his eyelids flutter, "Just know I love you, *cerecita*. That part was never a lie."

Clutching his near lifeless hand to my chest, I scream at the other men in the room, "Fucking do something!"

As though my screams are silent, they all ignore me. The three of them continuing to try to stop the blood from pumping out of Alex's body.

"No, Alex!" I squeeze his hand and pound it against my chest before releasing it.

As though I have no control over myself, my hand comes down hard against Alex's face. The slap echoing through the near empty room as it leaves a red mark across his cheek. Andres grips my arms and pulls me from Alex, but I fight against his hold, and he releases me.

Stepping back to Alex, I slap him again.

"You don't get to fucking die. Do you hear me?" My tearful words are filled with anger, "You don't get to fucking die and leave me like this."

I smack him again and again, as tearful demands continue to spill from my lips. I yell at him until I am no longer physically able to continue and my exhausted body collapses to my knees.

His face next to mine, I gently wrap my arms around him and press my face to his. Sobbing, my tears roll down his face as much as they do mine.

"You can't leave me, baby," I whisper into his ear, "We need you."

twenty five

ISABELLA

It's been three days since Andres pulled me downstairs to find Alex bleeding out on a kitchen table. Three long days filled with tears and sleepless nights. Countless hours spent looking back over our relationship wondering if I'd missed any hints at this whole other life he's been living. A whole other life I've been in the dark about.

While we have all cleaned this apartment, the metallic scent of blood still hangs in the air. Just now, it is masked with the scent of industrial cleaners. Eduardo removed and disposed of the bloodied carpet. I've scrubbed this table a countless number of times, but I can still feel the sticky residue of blood on it.

Regardless, this is where I have sat, cried, and tried to sleep for the past three days. Alex's men have tried desperately to get me to go up to the penthouse. Pleading with me to try to get some rest in my bed, or even a shower to clean up. But I cannot bring myself to leave this apartment.

"*Señora*," Andres startles me when he places his hand on my shoulder. Lifting my head from my hands, he slides an orange juice and a bagel in front of me. "It's been days. You need to eat something."

"I can't," my voice is pained and sounds strained from the days of crying, "I feel like I died."

"*Señora*, I need you to eat," he gently begs me, "Boss will have my ass when he wakes up if he finds out we didn't take care of you."

"Look at him," my arms gesture to the mattress from the penthouse on the floor, "It's been three days and he's barely moved."

"It's been three days and he's still alive," Andres nudges the bottle of juice in front of me, "I've been with him since we were kids at Saint Francis."

"Saint Francis?"

"The orphanage," he continues with a look on face like he knows he's sharing things he shouldn't, "after his family."

His eyes turn to Alex, and he swallows hard, "We are brothers. It might not be by blood, but he is my brother. He has taken care of me since we were kids, and there is nothing that I would not do for him."

Caught up in the story he is telling, I've eaten half of my bagel before I realize I even had it in my hand.

"I would give my life for him," he continues, "I would more than happily be the one lying on that mattress if it meant that he was okay."

"Shut the fuck up," a whispered groan comes from the floor, "this shit hurts like fucking hell and you wouldn't make it five minutes."

"Alex," I squeal, running to him. I drop down on the mattress way harder than I probably should, based on the loud groan Alex makes.

"*Cerecita*," he struggles to lift his hand and place it on my face, "*mi amor*."

My eyes close and my face melts into his hand, relishing in the indescribable relief I feel from him waking up. Opening my eyes, my hand slaps across his face and he grunts.

"Don't you ever fucking do that to me again," I yell at him as he struggles to smirk back up at me.

"I'm sorry," his thumb gently strokes the tear falling down my cheek.

"You don't get to convince me to marry you and make me fall in love you," I hold his hand against my face, "and then go and die on me. You are a man of your word, and you promised me a lifetime of firsts and lasts."

"*Cerecita,*" his voice pained as he continues to wipe the tears from my face, "It's going to take more than a couple of bullets to take me from you."

"You also don't get to make me fall in love with you while you live a double life," I move his hand to my stomach, "I'm not raising a child with a man who can't be honest with me."

His eyes soften and a single tear rolls from his eye. I swipe it with my thumb before anyone else has the opportunity to see this moment of weakness in him.

Using what little strength he has, Alex pulls me down to him and struggles to lift his head to kiss me.

"I'm so sorry," he mumbles against my lips.

"I will tell you everything. *Prometo,*" his words trail off as he begins to fall back asleep.

Sliding down on the mattress, I carefully press my body against his side as I lay my head on his chest. For the first time in three days, my heart doesn't feel broken. The vise that I'd felt around my chest has been loosened. I feel like I can breathe.

Listening to the slow, steady thump of Alex's heart pounding out the sounds of life, I finally fall asleep.

twenty six

ALEJANDRO

"Slow down," Isabella orders, "You're going to tear your stitches."

She probably isn't wrong, as I groan in pain trying to sit up on the makeshift bed.

El Doctor checks my wounds to ensure I am healing without issues. After providing me with some painkillers, that I won't take, he gives me the okay to get up and move around. Barring, of course, that I take it easy. Making it very clear that I am to have no physical exertion for at least a week.

The moment he leaves us, Isabella sits down on the mattress, stares at me with those huge green eyes of hers and says, "Spill it."

When I don't begin talking immediately, the look on her face quickly grows impatient.

I know it's wrong, but she's fucking adorable when she's mad at me.

"I gave you four days," she crosses her arms, "Now tell me everything."

"I was unconscious for three and a half of them," I quip.

"That sounds like a you problem," she snarks, "now start fucking talking."

I don't know what I would've done if I was wrong about her finding out.

Or what I'll do if she loses it when she hears the whole truth, because I refuse to live my life without her.

Or my child she's carrying inside her.

She listens in near silence as I tell her everything. That my real name is Alejandro Diaz. The brutal murder of my family. The years I spent at the boys' home, where I met Andres. How the two of us conspired to get vengeance on the men that killed my family. That in killing all of those men, I resumed my birthright, and I am the unknown head of the Diaz Cartel. I am relieved that she is still sitting beside me when I finish.

Even if she does look angry.

"Why didn't you tell me?" Her tone sounds more hurt than angry.

"I don't exactly walk around introducing myself as head of the cartel," I poorly try to make light of the situation, "You are one of five people who know who I really am."

"Who are the others?" She looks slighted.

"Andres, Eduardo, El Doctor, and my attorney."

I watch as she mulls over my answer for a minute.

"I understand why you didn't tell me when we first met," she hesitates, "But why not before we got married? Giving me the opportunity to choose if this is a life I wanted."

Would you have changed your mind?

As much as I want to, I don't answer. I know she needs to get out her feelings.

"Or after we'd been married for a year," she suddenly looks even more hurt, "When you knew you could trust me. Or did you not trust that I would keep your secret?"

Reaching out to her, I grunt through the pain as I grab her waist and pull her onto my lap. With her straddling my legs, I cup her face and stare into her eyes.

"*Cerecita,* do not think for even a minute that I would not trust you with my life."

"Then why?" Her lip trembles and I watch as the tears pool in the corners of her eyes.

"You are the most perfect, kind-hearted and unblemished person in my life," I catch the tear falling down her face with my thumb, "The only thing in my life not tarnished with violence and death. I didn't want to be the person to take that from you."

"That wasn't your decision to make, Alex. You may be my husband, but you do not have the right to hide things from me that could gravely affect my life."

She leans back and I grab her waist harder, fearing that she is going to get up. Instead, taking me by surprise, the palm of her hand crashes across my face.

"I love you. I will always fucking love you," her hand grips my jaw just below where she struck me, "but don't you ever fucking lie to me about anything ever again."

I smirk back at her. While I know it's only going to further infuriate her, I cannot help myself, "You're so fucking cute when you're mad at me."

Pulling her closer, I press my lips against hers and slide my tongue into her mouth. She takes it willingly and wrestles against it with her own. My cock grows beneath her, as though it's drawn to the warmth of her cunt. Feeling it, she grinds her hips against me, rubbing herself up and down the length of my shaft.

Both of us breathing heavy, she pulls back from our kiss.

"Never fucking lie to me again, Alex."

"Never, *cerecita*."

"Good," she climbs from my lap, "Andres will be down in a few minutes to help you upstairs."

"What the fuck am I supposed to do with this?" I point at the tented sheet where her lap used to be.

She shrugs as she walks out the door, calling back, "See you upstairs, baby."

twenty seven

ISABELLA

Flipping through the hangers in my closet, I settle on a cute, little T-shirt dress. Dropping my towel, I forgo undergarments and pull it over my head.

It's a little childish, but I've spent the last few days tormenting Alex. Wearing his favorite negligées to bed and parading around the house panty-free in short, little dresses.

It's amazing the number of things I keep dropping in front of him.

Apparently I'm such a klutz.

My actual anger with him was short-lived. Most of it had passed, while talking to Andres, in the days I thought I was going to lose Alex. While he didn't tell me everything, he had told me enough that I had time to process things.

Although I was truly upset that he withheld such a significant thing from me, I also understand why he did it. He truly was trying to protect me. If things went wrong, there truly was nothing to connect me to that aspect of his life.

I love him for wanting to keep me safe.

Hearing him share every last detail of his secret life to me only solidified that. Even though most people would probably have freaked out learning that their husband has killed numerous men, that part surprisingly didn't faze me.

I was never oblivious and have always known that Alex has a darker side to him. I saw it the first night that we met. It has shown itself in bits and pieces throughout our marriage, but never once toward me. There is nothing I could do to cause this man to lay a harmful hand on me.

Shit! He fucking smirked at me when I slapped him across the face.

Heading downstairs, I hear Alex on the phone in his office. I head to his office, after stopping in the kitchen to get him a cup of coffee. Walking to his side of the desk and placing the cup in front of him, I place a gentle kiss by his ear and whisper, "Good morning, baby."

Considering he is still on the call and not wanting to interrupt, I turn to leave. His hand grabs my wrist, and he pulls me back onto his lap with a yelp.

He mutes the call before firmly gripping my jaw and turning my face to his.

"I've had just about enough of this shit," he growls at me, "Fucking teasing me. Taunting me. Day and night."

Keeping his grip on my jaw and staring into my eyes, he pulls me to his face as his free hand slides up my thigh.

"I'm still mad at you," I snarl against his lips.

"You might be mad at me," his whispers back against my lips as his hand slides under my dress until his fingers brush along my pussy, "but your cunt isn't."

Kissing me, he slides a finger inside of me and I moan into his mouth. While it has only been about a week, it feels like it has been an eternity since he's touched me.

"I know you aren't really mad at me," he slides his finger up and down my slit, "Now, are you?"

Continuing to gently slide the pad of his finger over my clit, his lips and teeth travel the length of my neck until I cannot help but lean into him.

"It's been too long, *cerecita*," he whispers through the kisses he continues to plant on my neck, "The doctor told me I shouldn't fuck you yet, not that I can't."

His finger continues to slowly work in and out of me, teasing me and leaving me needing so much more from him.

"Now be quiet, like a good little girl, while I finish this call," he unmutes the phone and then whispers in my ear, "and then I'll let you ride my cock."

As he discusses the events of the past week over with whoever he is talking to, he adds another finger and continues his slow teasing pace. Occasionally he increases his speed or curl against my walls, leaving me biting my lower lip to stifle my cries.

"Do we have any idea who tipped off the DEA or what they know?" He stares at me as he talks to the man on the other end of the phone.

"It was an anonymous tip," the man on the other end responds, "I'm still looking into it. I don't know yet if it came from inside or a rival cartel."

"I need you to find out," his fingers work faster as he adds his thumb to my clit, "I will not put my family in danger because we can't find out where this threat is."

"It's my top priority, boss," the other man suddenly sounds a little afraid.

And Alex's authority is fucking hot as hell.

He hisses when I bite his shoulder, my hips writhing on his leg as he brings me right to the edge.

Placing a finger to his lips as a reminder for me to be quiet, his fingers curl vigorously inside of me as his thumb grinds over my clit. My hips twitching with every movement he makes; I struggle hard not to come. Knowing that when I do, it's going to come with a scream.

"Are you still mad at me?" he whispers against my ear.

I violently shake my head, unable to open my mouth to answer him.

"Good," he whispers.

Watching me tremble and shake on his lap on makes him more aggressive.

"We'll talk tomorrow," Alex abruptly interrupts the man on the other end, "I need to help my wife with something.

Smirking at me, he ends the call.

twenty eight

ALEJANDRO

"I know what my dirty little girl needs," I bite on her collarbone while relentlessly working her cunt with my fingers.

She is a trembling and writhing mess, clawing at my shoulders. She tightens around my fingers and screams through her release.

Pulling my fingers from her, I bring them up to her mouth. She needily sticks out her tongue to clean herself from me, and I rub my fingertips on her eager tongue.

"And I'll always make sure my dirty little girl gets exactly what she needs," I take my fingers into my mouth and suck the sweet taste of her from me.

"Fuck," I groan as I pull them from my mouth, "I've missed the taste of you on my tongue."

Pulling at my belt buckle and zipper, I open my pants. My hard cock is already dripping with pre-cum when I pull it from my pants.

"As much as I want to lick you from ass to cunt," I drag her from my thigh and place my tip against her entrance, "I want to bury my cock inside of you more."

Pulling her backward, I drag her over my length until I'm balls deep inside of her.

"Fuck," I groan against the back of her neck, "Your warm, wet cunt feels so fucking good around my cock."

Her feet planted between mine and her hands on my thighs, she grinds her ass against my lap. She rides me hard, trying desperately to bring herself over the edge again.

"That's it," My hands slide under her dress and firmly grip each of her tits. Squeezing them and toying with each of her nipples, her head falls back onto my shoulder as she continues to work herself over my length.

"Take what you need from me," I flex my hips, grinding back up into her, "Show me how much you missed my cock."

"I missed having you inside of me," she breathlessly moans.

"I know, *cerecita*," I pull at her nipples, "You're so fucking wet for me, I can feel your sweet fucking arousal dripping down my balls."

"Alex," she groans my name, and it sounds like fucking heaven.

"Does it feel good? Having my cock stretch out your tight, little cunt."

"Yes!"

"Are you going to come all over my cock to show me?"

She doesn't answer. Instead, she works her hips faster as she rubs her clit until I can feel her trembling and quivering around my cock.

"Fuck," I groan against her, "You feel so fucking good when you come."

I hold her against my chest as she rides out the last waves of her orgasm.

Wrapping my arm around her waist, I thrust into her as I stand the two of us up from the chair. I swipe my free arm across the desk and push the coffee, phone and other items in front of us to the floor before bending her over the desk.

"That tight little asshole of yours would look so fucking good with my cum dripping from it," I firmly palm her ass. Sliding my cock up and down her wet slit, I ensure to tease her clit with it. "You'd like that, wouldn't you?"

"Yes," her ass presses back to me.

"So needy to have me back inside of you," I slide my cock back into her cunt and press my thumb into her mouth. When I pull it back out, it is slick with my saliva.

"I don't have any lube," I rub my wet thumb against her tight little hole, "You're going to have to settle for my cock in your cunt and my thumb in your ass."

"Please," she begs while arching her ass further into the air.

Her begging always does me in, and I press my thumb into her tight little ass.

Fisting the dress at the nape of her neck, I pull it over her head, and she helps to remove it and tosses it to the floor. My hand slides up and down her bare spine, pushing her gently into the desk as my cock and thumb slowly thrust into her in unison.

"Hold the desk, *cerecita*," I growl down at her, and she grips her hands around the edge,

Gathering her hair in my fist and fighting through the pain in my side, I pull back and drive into her. Both of us grunting with each demanding thrust, as the desk slowly inches from its place. Isabella clenching around me tightly and my balls tightening with every blow, I know I'm not going to make it much longer.

"Fuck," I groan through my final thrust, plunging into the hilt as I unload my cum into her.

Carefully removing my thumb from her, she groans as though she still wants more. Keeping my cock inside of her cunt, I pull her onto my lap as I sit back in my chair.

"I'm not done with you," I hold her back to my chest as my fingers travel to her clit. Slowly and gently playing with her sensitive clit, "I intend to keep you coming on my lap until my cock grows hard inside of you. When it does, I'm going to fuck you again. Slow and deep as I whisper in your ear how much I fucking love you."

twenty nine

ISABELLA

"Are you sure you're ready to be out there already?" It's been three weeks since Alex was shot, but it still feels too soon for him to be back out there.

"Yes, *cerecita*," he grips my ass and pulls me tight to him, "With how I've been fucking you lately, you know damned well I'm just fine."

I can't argue.

He isn't wrong.

Wanting him to stay home has more to do with fear that something will go wrong again.

"Andres scheduled a meet with his man on the inside of the DEA," his tone is suddenly all business, "Even if I was still bleeding out, I'd need to be there."

I nod my head, knowing where this is going.

"Maintaining control in this world is all about power and fear," his fingers snake around my throat, "The moment you give a hint of weakness, someone will come for what you have."

Sliding his other hand through the hair at the nape of my neck, he fists it and pulls me into his mouth. His tongue plunging into my mouth as he kisses me until I can no longer breathe. Gently biting my lower lip between his teeth, he pulls away from me.

He leaves me unsteady and longing for him as he whispers against my lips, "And I'm not willing to let anyone take what is mine."

"Until I know what's going on," his hand pushes my chin up so that my eyes are on his, "I would prefer if you stayed at home. If you do leave, I want at least two men with you."

"Is that a request, baby? Or a demand?"

"It's a request," he softly kisses my forehead, "but Mateo and Luis downstairs might feel differently if you try to leave."

"Very funny."

"I will never joke about the safety of my family," his tone is very sincere.

"Well, I was planning on going out and doing a little shopping today. I know I still have a little time left still, but I'd like to have some clothes before I start outgrowing everything I own."

"Mmmm," Alex moans, "I love the idea of fucking you with a big round belly growing my child."

"You do know that you can't fuck another baby into me while I'm pregnant, right?" I half jest at him.

"Yes," he steps close to me again and leans down to my ear, "But that isn't going to stop me from filling you with my cum while I try."

His lips graze over my neck and suddenly my panties are soaked with need for him.

Pulling the neckline of my shirt to the side, his lips travel to my collarbone where he sucks gently until he leaves his mark on me.

Pressing into his lips, I moan, "Do you always have to do this to me before you go?"

"Do what, *cerecita*?" He plays coy.

The look on my face must speak volumes because the corner of his mouth ticks up as he arches an eyebrow at me.

"You know damned well," I playfully shove him away from me.

"I just like to make sure you're going to be thinking of me while I'm gone," he grabs his gun from the coffee table and tucks it into the waistband of his pants, "I'm sorry if that comes with wet panties."

"You're lucky I love you."

"I love you too, *cerecita*," I swear he winks at me as the elevator doors close between us.

Heading into the kitchen, I turn on some music. I pull out the coffee beans to make the sad, singular cup I'm allowed to have. The sound of the beans in the grinder echoes throughout the kitchen, drowning out Doja Cat blaring through the speaker.

As the grinder slows to a stop, I scream as I'm startled by a deep voice standing immediately behind me, "Where are they? Where are Alex and Andres?"

"Jesus fucking Christ, Eddie!" My breathing still heavy, "You scared the shit out of me."

"Don't call me Eddie," Eduardo's face and tone are serious, "Where the fuck are they?"

"Alex left for some meeting just a few minutes ago. I think he was going to the office," I don't know why I lie.

"Don't fucking lie to me," his hand grips my wrist painfully tight and I wince, "This is the third meeting they've had without me this week. Where the fuck did they go?"

The forcefulness of his grip and the look on his face has tears welling in the corner of my eyes.

"I don't know," my voice is pained, "I just know there was a meeting."

He uses the grip on my wrist to shove me away from him, and as quickly as he snuck in here, he's in the elevator, leaving. Rubbing my wrist and letting the tears roll down my face, I hear him mumble, "Useless fucking whore."

thirty

ALEJANDRO

It is pouring as we make our way through the city. Andres splashes through a puddle as he pulls the car to a stop under an empty overpass.

This meeting could not be any more cliché.

Looking at the time, we are about five minutes early as we climb from the car.

My phone buzzes in my pocket.

EDUARDO

Where's the meeting?

Andres and I have it handled

Why are you shutting me out?

You're being paranoid

He's not being paranoid.

Not entirely.

But the only two people in this world I trust wholeheartedly right now are my wife and my brother.

Shoving my phone back into my pocket, it vibrates again as another car pulls to a stop next to ours.

Andres nods his head at me, acknowledging that the man in the car is the one we are supposed to be meeting with.

As he climbs from the car, I feel my phone buzz again.

"What is this shit?" He looks both me and Andres up and down, "You get to know who I am, but I don't get to see your faces?"

"No one sees my face," my words are muffled through the mask pulled over my head, "Ever."

I watch him fidget nervously for a moment, it's quite apparent that he is determining whether or not he wants to stay.

"I just want to know about the raid at the shipyard," I lean back against the side of my car, trying to appear less of a threat. "How did the DEA know about the shipment?"

"You have an informant in your organization."

"A fucking narc?" Andres exclaims before I have a chance.

"I have information," the agent slowly and carefully pulls an envelope from the breast pocket of his suit jacket. Then very nervously says, "but I want twenty grand."

Gesturing at Andres, he pops the trunk of the car and returns with a thick manilla envelope.

"This is fifty," I shake the envelope at him, "You tell me everything you know. You answer when A calls. And you make sure we never get hit like that again."

"How am I supposed to do that?"

"You seem to be a smart guy," I walk closer to him and place the envelope in his hand, still holding onto it firmly, "You'll figure that out."

"Does the DEA know who I am?"

"No," he shakes his head in unison with his response, "he hasn't given that information over yet."

"What do they know?"

"Just that you live between New York and Mexico," his fingers grip the envelope in his palm, "and no one knows what you look like."

"Do you know who my snitch is?"

My phone buzzes in my pocket again.

"All communication to this point has been anonymous. The DEA doesn't know his name or what he looks like."

"Then what's the envelope?" I snatch it from his hand while simultaneously letting go of the envelope of money.

"It's a USB of the recorded calls that led to the raid at the shipyard," he nervously pulls the money close to his chest.

"And you think this is worth twenty grand?" Andres snidely asks him.

"All of them are date and time stamped," the agent fidgets nervously.

"He knows things. He's not some low-level guy," he begins to ramble, "I thought..."

"You thought what?" I curtly interrupt him.

"In one of them, there's a woman in the background," he swallows hard, "and she calls him Eddie."

My eyes dart to Andres as the agent continues to speak, "And I figured you would know his voice."

I don't need to listen to it. Isabella calls him that because she knows it annoys him.

"If we call, you fucking answer," I stare at him," Understood?"

"Yes," he nervously nods his head quickly.

By the time I finish with the agent, Andres is already in the driver's seat and has the engine running.

Andres has the car in drive by the time I shut my door.

Needing to alert security, I pull my phone from my pocket. I am surprised to find the many messages during the meeting weren't from Eduardo. They're from Isabella.

ISABELLA

Something is wrong

Eddie was just here

Baby, he scared me

Where are you?

Alex?

I need you…

Are you okay?

I'm calling security now

And I'm on my way

He just came back

I'm scared

Getting shot and nearly dying didn't faze me. The thought of anything happening to the woman I love physically hurts.

thirty one

ISABELLA

Pacing the kitchen with my phone in hand, I wait anxiously for Alex to text me back.

He never ignores my texts.

Ever.

Alex?

I need you…

If anything happened to him…

Are you okay?

I'm calling security now

Thank God…

And I'm on my way

The elevator dings and I hear the doors slide open.

That's too soon to be Alex...

Moving to the other side of the island so that I can see into the foyer, my heart stops when I see it's Eddie. Quickly walking back to the other side of the island to but a barrier between us, I text Alex back.

He just came back

I'm scared

I no more than send the text as Eddie is approaching the other side of the island. I didn't notice earlier, but he is a mess. Especially for a man that usually takes a lot of pride in his appearance. His hair is disheveled, he hasn't shaved, and his eyes are bloodshot.

Reaching the island, he places his left hand on the countertop. When he does the same with his right, I step back and swallow hard at the sight of the gun. Staring at me, he intimidatingly taps the gun on the marble.

And fuck, does it ever work.

"Time to go, sweetheart," his words ice through my veins.

"I'm not going anywhere with you, Eddie."

"Don't fucking call me Eddie," he seethes at me, "And I'm not fucking asking."

Assuming he won't shoot me, I dart from where I stand and pull a chef's knife from the butcher block. When I turn from the counter, Eddie is standing only a few feet from me.

"What do you plan to do with that? Make me a fucking sandwich?"

The knife trembles in my grip as I swipe it in his direction. He hisses when I make contact with his arm. Blood drips from his wound, but it only infuriates him.

Lunging at me, the back of his hand comes down hard across my cheek. The pain of his strike radiates through my face and eye, causing me to cry out in pain. Shoving my disoriented body backward, I hit the counter as he pulls the knife from my hand and tosses it to the floor.

I cringe as his bloody fingers curl around my throat, squeezing hard enough to impede my ability to breathe. Struggling to suck in air, I forcefully lift my knee into his crotch.

The blow catches him off-guard, and he lets go of my throat to clutch at his manhood. Pushing away from the counter, I run with all of my might toward the elevator.

If I can just get to the guards downstairs in the garage...

As my barefoot steps over the threshold to the elevator, Eddie fists the hair at the back of my head and yanks me backward. He pulls so hard that I'm brought to the ground in tears.

"Get up, bitch," he uses my hair as leverage to pull me from the ground.

My feet scrambling beneath me, I struggle to stand to alleviate the pain caused from him pulling at my hair.

"I'd recommend against trying that shit again," he pushes the button to take us down to the garage with the muzzle of the gun, his other hand still firmly gripping my hair.

Feeling the elevator coming to a stop, I scream for help. Hoping that my screams alert the men on the other side of the door that there is a situation. The doors open and Eddie chuckles as he shoves me forward by my hair.

"They aren't going to help you," he pushes me past the guards. Both are sitting on the ground, beneath a trail of blood smeared down the wall they are both now slumped lifelessly against.

The concrete of the garage is cold and hard against my bare feet, only increasing the pain of every forced step.

Popping the trunk of the car, he shoves me toward it and waves the gun in my direction, "Get in."

"Eddie," I look up at him, "You don't have to do this."

"Get in the fucking trunk, sweetheart."

Even with the gun waving in my face, my body won't move.

If he's going to kill me, it can happen here.

With the gun in his hand, he punches me in the face, and everything immediately goes fuzzy.

"I said get in the fucking trunk," I feel him shove my crumpling body as everything goes black.

thirty two

ALEJANDRO

Andres is speeding, swerving around cars, taking red lights, and doing whatever he can. Regardless, he can't make it through city traffic fast enough for me and he knows it.

The phone lines are down for the building, and I can't reach security. Redialing Isabella, I slam my fist into the dash when it goes to voicemail yet again.

My heart is thumping in my throat, and my fist crashes into the dash again and again. I need to vent out of some of this anger...and fear.

Andres stays silent, his eyes focused on the road and getting us back to the penthouse. He's known me long enough to know that words won't console me right now.

Finally pulling into the garage, it's quiet. No different from any other Tuesday morning.

"That's Eduardo's car," Andres gestures to his left before pulling us to a stop near the elevators. My stomach drops when I see two of my men slumped over on the ground.

Climbing from the car, I run the distance to the elevator and slam my palm repeatedly against the call button. Bending down while I wait for the doors to open, I check the men on the ground for pulses and pull the guns from their holsters.

When the doors open, Andres and I quickly run inside, and I hand him one of the guns.

"I want him alive," the tone of my voice is feral, "but if you have to, don't hesitate to kill him."

"Understood," Andres watches the floors tick by with me, preparing to rush from this elevator the moment the doors open to the penthouse.

The elevator dings and the doors slide open to complete silence in the penthouse. Andres makes his way through the main floor while I check unsuccessfully upstairs.

"Alex!" Andres calls for me from downstairs with a tinge of fear in his voice.

Taking the stairs two at a time, I can't get down them fast enough. When I reach the landing and see him standing in the kitchen, the look on his face turns my stomach.

My brain is telling me to run to get there quickly, but my heart is terrified what I am going to find. I can barely move my feet to cross the living room and it feels like I am walking in slow motion.

"She's not here," relief washes over me at Andres words.

The brief moment of consolation is taken from me the second I step into the kitchen. The floor is scattered with blood – drips, smears, and footprints. The partial footprints are a mixture of a large man's boot and Isabella's tiny bare feet.

Making my way through the kitchen, I see Isabella's phone on the counter. Picking it up, I swipe it open to see our text conversation.

He just came back

I'm scared

It is the unsent one that sends me over the edge.

Baby I love y

"*Maldito hijo de puta,*" I slam her phone to the ground in anger, shattering it to pieces. My hands grabbing anything I can reach on the counters; I continue to scream profanities while throwing things against the wall and floor.

When there are no more items to throw, my hands grip the edge of the counter. Squeezing it so hard with my hands that my arms and body begin shaking, I release an animalistic roar.

Walking from the kitchen, I place my fist through the wall by the archway as I make my way to the stairs. Violently, I storm up the steps and barge into the bedroom, heading straight to the closet.

Stripping out of my suit, I pull on a pair of dark jeans and a black long-sleeved t-shirt. Sitting at the edge of the bed while I pull on my boots, Andres appears in the doorway.

"What are you doing?" His question simply causes me annoyance.

"Going to fucking get Isabella," I snarl at him.

Stepping into the bedroom, Andres begins shedding his dress clothes while walking to my closet. He emerges pulling on a pair of my jeans and a navy t-shirt, with a pair of my boots in his hand.

"What are you doing?" I question him.

"Fucking going with you, *hermano*."

"You don't even know where I'm going."

"It doesn't matter," Andres places his hand on my shoulder and squeezes it firmly, "You know I'll follow you into battle anywhere."

I do know...

Since we were kids, protecting each other from those that came at us, we're bonded closer than most blood brothers. Both of us would lay down our lives for the other.

Heading back downstairs, I grab my phone and pull up Eduardo's number.

> I know you have my cerecita
>
> I am coming for you

I don't know where you are, but I am going to fucking end you.

thirty three

ISABELLA

My body being jostled jerks me awake.

The sun shining down on my face is so bright that it causes me to squint. The scrunching of my face causes me to wince in pain, and I vaguely remember Eddie hitting me in the face.

That pain is only made worse when he grabs my head and roughly pulls a gag through my mouth before tying it behind my head. Trying to use my hands to fight him off, I realize that they are bound behind my back.

Gripping my shoulders, Eddie pulls me upright. The abrupt motion makes me dizzy and nauseous. I nearly vomit when he throws me over his shoulder. A feeling that only intensifies when his hand grips my ass.

The ways I hope to God that it is just so he doesn't drop me.

Struggling against the urge to go back to sleep, I try to look around to see where we are.

"Wheels up in five minutes," Eddie commands to someone I can't see. Before I even see it, I realize we are at the air terminal.

Fuck.

Where is he taking me?

Still slung over his shoulder, my body is jostled around with every step he takes. With my limbs bound, there is nothing I can do to brace myself as I repeatedly bounce against him.

Every step feels like he has taken me miles from my Alex.

Carrying me up the steps, he walks me onto the Learjet, and roughly drops me into a seat. Looking around as he fastens my seatbelt, I don't know if I feel relief or fear over the fact that we are alone.

Probably an equal amount of both.

He paces the aisle of the plane and pulls a snuff bullet from his pocket. Fiddling with it for a moment, he brings it to his nose and inhales deeply.

Fuck...

Unhinged and high.

Continuing to pace the short length of the airplane, he is incoherently rambling to himself. Occasionally I catch bits and pieces of what he's saying, but I'm not able to piece it together.

The look in his eyes as he approaches me is terrifying. Leaning down, he strokes the back of his fingers down my face and along my jaw. His touch causing every hair on the back of my neck to stand on end.

"Do you remember the last time I was on a plane with you?" The sudden calmness in his voice is eerie.

My mind is fuzzy, but I don't recall being on a flight with him. I've flown with Alex and Andres a few times to Mexico, but usually it's just me and Alex.

Shaking my head, he snickers.

"Were you faking it for him?" He continues to sneer.

My confusion must be written across my face, because only seems to become more agitated at me.

"The last time I flew with you, sweetheart. The day after you an Alejandro first met" his tone is snide, "We all listened to you scream for an hour as he fucked you."

His fingers continuing to trail down my arm, my entire body stiffens with my repulsion.

"So, tell me," his fingers continue to slide up and down the bare skin of my arm, "Were you faking it for him? To make him feel like more of man?"

A tear rolling down my cheek, my lips trembling around the gag in my mouth, I shake my head at him.

"Do you think you'd scream that loud for me?" I swallow down the bile in the back of my throat, "If I fucked you with that gag in your mouth."

Tears now rolling down my face, I try to beg him not to touch me. My muffled words fill the small aircraft as the sound of tearful moans.

His eyes are slowly drawn to the cleavage at the neckline of my tank top, his hands following not far behind.

This isn't fucking happening.

Eddie's hand roughly cups my breast when he is distracted by the phone ringing in his pocket. Standing up abruptly, he pulls his phone out and paces again as he reads it.

"Apparently your big, bad husband wants you back," he flashes the text messages in my direction.

ALEJANDRO

I know you have my cerecita

I am coming for you

Alex...

Baby....

Firmly gripping the hair at the top of my head, he yanks my head back and takes a photo of me. Typing rapidly on the phone, I hear him send several more messages before he puts it back into his pocket.

"Since he ruined the mood," Eddie shrugs his shoulders, "I guess we'll just have to relive a different moment from that flight."

My eyes widen, remembering I slept most of that flight and don't know what else happened on it.

Just as panic is beginning to pump through my body, I see Eddie's elbow rushing toward my face.

thirty four

ALEJANDRO

Stuffing duffel bags with everything we might need from the armory, Eduardo finally messages me back.

The first text that comes through is a picture of Isabella. Her eye and temple are bruised and bloody, her hair matted and stuck to her face from where she was cut. She has a gag in her mouth, that appears to be tied painfully tight. I can almost feel the pain and fear radiating from her eyes.

His death is going to be slow and extremely fucking painful.

> EDUARDO
>
> You want her, come and get her
>
> It's going to cost you

Tell me where

Los Cangrejos

"Call the pilot, Andres. We're going to Mexico."

I'll send you the address

But I want everything else you have

I don't know what the fuck that means, but I'll give fucking anything to get her back.

And he knows it.

Stowing everything in the trunk, Andres drives us through the city toward the airfield. While he drives, I text the resort manager in Cabo San Lucas to let them know to get my villa ready.

My next text goes out to the men who run my warehouses in Los Cangrejos, complete with pictures of Eduardo and Isabella's battered face.

There are only so many places to hide in Los Cangrejos, motherfucker.

And I own most of them.

It has only been a couple of hours since Isabella was taken from the penthouse. At most, they will only land in Mexico a few hours before us.

The inability to do virtually anything makes the flight to Mexico feel unimaginably long, and I am happy when we finally land and I can be productive again.

Well, as happy as I can be.

Walking to my hangar, Andres pulls out with the Land Rover. Once he parks it by the plane, we unload the bags of weapons. Pulling two masks from the bags, we climb into the front seat.

"Head to the warehouses first," I direct Andres, "If there is even the smallest chance Eduardo has turned some of our men, I'm not waiting to find out."

"Our men?" He questions.

"You know damned well that while this is my father's legacy," I turn toward him, "You are my brother and you have helped me build it into the empire that it is."

"Alejandro..."

"It's not a discussion. You've been making an equal share of profits with me since the beginning."

He looks at me with a hint of surprise on his face.

"Considering you're willing to give your life not just to save mine, but to get me back the woman I love, I figured you should know just how important you are to me."

"Do I need to pull over?" Andres turns to me and gestures to the side of the road.

"What for?"

"I wasn't sure if you wanted to hug me or suck my cock while you were at it," he bats his eyes at me.

"*Que te jodan.*"

"Love you too, brother."

We are just a few blocks from the warehouse when I pull my mask over my head. Grabbing the wheel, I steer momentarily so that Andres can pull his on as well.

Pulling up to the warehouse, the two men standing guard open the gate to allow us access.

"El jefe," Rafael calls to me the moment we step from the SUV, "We were not expecting you."

"I know," my tone serious, "Is he here?"

"The man from the pictures?" He questions, "No, Jefe. He has not been here."

"If you see him or if E contacts you, you need to call me immediately. Understand."

"Si," he nods his head at me.

Andres and I make similar visits at our warehouses in Legunitas and El Caribe, taking brief walks through each packing facility. Upon leaving all of them, the two of us are more than satisfied that while Eduardo may be working with someone, he has not turned any of my cartel against me.

As much as I want to go through Los Cangrejos door by door looking for Isabella, I know Andres is right when he convinces me to head to the villa at the resort.

"I know it's going to be hard, if not impossible," Andres grabs one of the bags from the back of the SUV, "but you need to eat something and try to get some sleep."

He isn't wrong, I need to be rested to go after Eduardo, so I can get my cerecita back.

thirty five

ISABELLA

Struggling to breathe, I groan as I come to. My whole face hurts and feels swollen, and breathing feels stuffy like I have a horrible cold. My mouth is dry, and I have a faint metallic taste on my tongue

That fucking asshole hit me in the face again.

How long was I out?

I struggle to open my eyes and a moment of panic hits when I realize that I am no longer on the plane.

Where the fuck am I?

As I struggle to lift my head, I realize how cold and hard the floor is beneath me. Pulling my head from my chest, I rest it against the wooden post I'm leaning against. Trying to move, I realize I'm not leaning against the post.

I'm tied to it.

Pulling my hands and trying to lower my arms, my wrists burn. Both are already sore and tender from where the rope pulled and rubbed while I was unconscious. I wrap my hands around the rope binding me to the post in hopes that I will alleviate the pain.

The only source of light is coming from the single bulb hanging from the ceiling not far above my head. The cold floor beneath me is concrete. All the walls I can see are brick, and there are no windows.

A basement.

I must be in a basement.

No one is going to stumble across me here.

Tears of sheer hopelessness trickle down my face. I sob, and the pain it causes only makes me cry harder. I try unsuccessfully to stifle my cries, and for the first time I am thankful for the gag in my mouth. It will silence my cries and hopefully not draw Eddie's attention to me.

My hopes are short lived when I hear the distinctive creak of wooden stairs behind me. Every muscle in my body tightens as I hear footsteps approaching behind me.

"It's almost time to reach out to your husband," his voice is close, and he must be standing right behind me, "And we need to get you cleaned up."

The sound of that turns a knot in my stomach.

"I'm going to remove the gag," his tone is gruff, "If you scream, you will fucking regret it. Do you understand?"

Tears still trickling down my face, I nod in agreement.

Eddie unties the gag and pulls it from my mouth. Searing fire burns through my jaw as I try to stretch the muscles in my face.

Leaving the rope bound around my wrists, he unties it from the post and uses it to pull me to my feet. My body is struggling to keep up as he pulls me across the basement. While I don't know how my legs will struggle to climb them, I'm hoping he drags me up them.

Maybe if I scream, someone will hear me.

Instead, he drags me to a shower in the corner. More correctly, a showerhead with a drain in the floor beneath it. Holding the rope with one hand, he pulls a box cutter from his back pocket.

"Behave," he flicks the blade out, "or I will hurt you."

My breathing stutters as fear surges through me, followed by silent sobs as he slowly cuts through the fabric of my tank top and my shorts. Tossing the fabric to the ground, his eyes roam over my semi-covered body for a moment before he pulls the razor blade through the lacy fabric of my bra and panties.

His eyes continue to look over my body, and with my bound wrists I am not able to do much to try and cover myself.

Eddie turns the water on, and I screech as icy, cold water washes over my body. Every inch of my skin is suddenly covered in goosebumps, and I am trembling.

Shoving a bar of soap in my hands, Eddie grunts, "Clean up."

I immediately do as he asks, hoping that it will get me out from under this freezing cold water. Lathering the bar of soap in my hands, I drag it over my icy skin.

A groan coming from Eddie draws my attention to him, and I swallow hard when I find him palming his erection through his pants.

This isn't happening...

"It's a shame I don't have time for you right now," he turns off the water and drags my dripping and shivering body back to the post. Securing me to it, his fingers trail down my naked torso, "But I'm going to find time for you later."

"You don't have to do this, Eddie," the sympathetic sounding words blurt from my mouth.

The instep of his foot kicks me in the stomach, knocking the air out of me, and leaving me struggling to breathe.

"I've told you several times," he leans down and firmly grips my already sore face, "Not to call me Eddie."

Releasing me, he steps backward. He pulls his phone from his pocket and snaps several photos of me.

"Time to go find out how much your husband really loves you," he smirks as he tucks his phone back into his pocket.

The cold water from my hair continues to run down my torso, my whole body trembles, as I listen to the creak of the stairs.

I try to curl my body tight in an attempt to get warm. My face resting on my knees, I sob silently against my cold flesh.

thirty six

ALEJANDRO

The phone buzzing in my hand startles me. I must have dozed off sometime early this morning waiting for more info on Isabella.

Lifting the phone, my teeth clench and I growl when I swipe it open to find a picture of Isabella. She is naked. Battered and bruised. And tied up like a fucking animal.

Being treated like a fucking animal because of me.

Breathing hard, my jaw clenched so tight it's painful. I continue through the messages.

EDUARDO

Your wife is quite beautiful

If you lay a fucking hand on her I'll
kill you

You'll be respectful and do as I say, or
I'll do far more than lay a hand on her

What do you want

Do you love your wife Alejandro?

Of course I love my wife

Do you love her more than your
empire?

Yes

I'm going to need you to prove it.

Your empire for her life

Try to fuck me and I'll have her
smacked out while all of Mexico takes
a try at her little pink, gringo cunt

I will give you whatever you want

The mere thought of Isabella being passed into the skin trade has me seeing red. She is strong as hell, but that's not a life that any woman can endure.

There are not words to describe the slow, brutal death Eduardo is about to endure.

St. Francis

Ninety minutes

Come alone

"He's going to kill you," Andres is the first of us to speak.

"I know," the words come through my still gritted teeth. "He has to. It's the only way he can assume control, by taking it with force."

"Saint Francis is a trap," Andres paces, "It's an hour from here. It won't give us any time to prepare. He'll be there waiting."

Andres is right.

I'm willingly walking, no running, to my death.

Pulling off my shirt, I unzip the duffel bag and pull out a Kevlar vest. Fastening the Velcro, I pull my shirt back over my head.

"That isn't going to do shit if he shoots you in the head," Andres pulls his from the duffle bag as well and puts it on over his shirt.

"Then one of us better get to him first," I pull two handguns from the bag and tuck them into the back of my pants. Andres does the same and also pulls out a Ruger AR-556.

"What?" He raises an eyebrow at me, "I like to be prepared."

"I'm going to take the Land Rover," I toss a set of keys to Andres, "You take the Jeep. It'll blend better and hopefully he won't see you coming."

Within minutes, the two of us are in our respective vehicles and barreling toward the outskirts of Todos Santos.

Saint Francis is a place both Andres and I thought we would never have to see or visit again. With all I've seen and experienced in this life, my years in that hell of a boys' home are some of the most prolific and painful.

The year Andres and I aged out and were placed on the streets, we freed the others from the brutality and abuse that happened behind those locked doors. A large fire destroyed the majority of the dormitories, resulting in the death of nearly all of the staff and clergy. The newspapers dubbed it a miracle that all of the children escaped without a single injury.

Yes.

A miracle.

When we are a few miles from Saint Francis, Andres's car drops back from me. Within minutes, I am no longer able to see him in my rearview mirror.

This will be the first time since the day I was brought here that I will be facing it without Andres by my side.

While the town of Todos Santos has grown over the years, construction never seems to come in the direction of this place. With the view of town in the distance, I pull up to the dilapidated remains of the building. The years have not been kind to it, but it is somehow still standing.

Rectifying that will be next on my list.

Parking the Land Rover in the overgrown parking lot, I exit the SUV and cautiously make my way to the front of the building. I pull one of the guns from my waistband, then I crack the front door. Peering inside and listening, I am hoping not to be hit with an ambush the moment I step inside.

Pushing it further, it swings open with the loud creak of a door that hasn't had its hinges oiled in decades.

thirty seven

ISABELLA

"Time to go, sweetheart," the sweetness in Eddie's voice makes me cringe as he stomps down the creaking steps.

Standing over me, he unties the rope from the post. I wince when he uses it to pull me to my feet. Since the make-shift shower, the tight, wet rope has nearly rubbed through my skin.

"Let's go," he pulls again. I wrap my hands around the taught rope between us hoping to alleviate some of the pull around my wrists.

Nearly dragging my naked body behind him, he pulls me up the stairs and down a few hallways in a dirty, rundown building. Darting my eyes around, I try to take in my surroundings.

Pushing open a door, he pulls me inside and shoves me into a chair. I breathe a moment of relief when he removes the rope from my wrists, both red, bruised, and bloody. He grips one, causing me to cry out, as he pulls it down roughly to the arm of the chair before using a zip tie to keep it in place. I place my other arm against the chair, in hopes that he won't grab this one as well.

"Look at you," he cinches the zip tie, "such a good girl. The boys are going to love you."

The boys?

Those two words elicit a fear in me unlike any I have ever felt before, and I don't know why.

Eddie bends down in front of me and roughly grabs my ankle, tying it to the leg of the chair. Squeezing my thighs and knees together, I try to keep him from doing the same with the other. Even if I wasn't bound to this chair, I am no match for his strength. Forcing my legs apart, he binds my other ankle to the chair.

My body recoils when he places his hands on my upper thighs, His head presses between my thighs and he takes a deep breath, letting out a moan as he stands in front of me.

"I am definitely getting a taste of that sweet cunt before I get rid of you," he licks his lips while adjusting the obvious erection in his pants. Slightly rubbing himself, he continues to stare at my body on display for him.

I spit at him, and his hand violently grips my chin, "Now now, sweetheart. Ladies don't spit. Besides, where you're going you are going to be expected to swallow."

My entire body shudders at his words.

I would rather die.

Letting go of my face, he steps back from me and looks at his watch.

"Not much longer now," he takes a bump from the snuff bullet he carries in his pocket, "How many women are this lucky?"

"Lucky?" I mumble back.

"You're about to learn if your husband actually loves you," he rubs at his nose, "or if he just keeps you around for that little pink cunt between your thighs."

He takes a second hit of drugs, and within minutes he is pacing and rambling erratically.

"He says he loves you," he pulls the gun from his pants, "but what man in his right mind would give up his empire – his family legacy – for a stupid fucking whore?"

I'm not a stupid fucking whore...

"He's been pushing me out for years. It's always been him and Andres," he rambles to me but more to himself, "But then you came along. Now I'll never be more than his number three. He'll never listen to me like he listens to Andres. Or to you."

"That's what this is about?" The words sputter from my mouth, "You took me because you want to take control?"

"It's more than that," he repeatedly taps his gun against his thigh, "He brought you into our inner sanctum. He didn't ask. Didn't care if you knew who we were. You took family from me."

I don't speak, my brain too overwhelmed trying to follow what he's saying.

"With you, I'll never be more than his number three," he waves his gun at me, "and with every fucking baby he puts in you I'll become less."

His eyes are red and crazed as he continues, "Why be his number three...or four...or five...when I can be El Jefe?"

"He's letting you take everything from me," he continues to rant, "So I'm going to take everything from him."

Eddie stalks toward me and shoves his gun into my stomach. My heart stops as he speaks, "Starting with his family."

A tear rolls down my cheek when he pulls the gun from my stomach.

"Pregnant whores don't make money," he smirks at me, "The men I'm giving you to will take care of that for me, so they can put you to work."

"I'm thinking I let Alejandro live for a little while," he strolls away from me, "bring him to visit you from time to time. Let him watch you get strung out and fucked by strangers all day."

I try, but I cannot control the tears.

thirty eight

ALEJANDRO

Making my way down these hallways has my skin crawling. A feeling that is only made worse when I begin to follow Eduardo's loud rambling rant.

Grabbing the phone from my back pocket, I shoot a few texts to Andres.

> They're in the gymnasium
>
> He's fucking high
>
> And he's fucking cracked

ANDRES

> Coming through the back
>
> Be there in 3 minutes

Pushing open the door, the hinges grind alerting Eduardo to my presence. By the time I am in the room, he is standing with his arm wrapped around Isabella's throat. His gun pressed firmly to her head, he is using her naked body as a shield.

Seeing what he has done to her, the only thing stopping me from putting a round through his skull is the possibility it could hit Isabella.

"Cerecita," her name painfully spills from my lips.

This situation she is in, it is my fault.

"Drop your gun," Eduardo dimples Isabella's temple with the muzzle of his gun.

"Don't, Alex," she grunts when he pushes harder, "He's going to kill you."

Releasing my hold on it, I let my gun fall in my palm before placing it on the ground.

"The other one too," he yells, "I know you never carry just one."

Slowly pulling the second from the waistband of my pants, I lower it to the ground as well.

"Kick them over here," Eduardo waves his gun at me, "And back away from them."

Nudging them both with my feet, I kick them a few feet in front of me and back away with my hands in the air.

"Where is your brother?" Eduardo eyes me suspiciously.

"I left him at the villa," I lie, "Snuck out when you text me."

"So, you came alone?"

Fucking hurry up, Andres.

"Yes. That's what you asked," my tone is steady, "It's just us."

"For now," his voice sounds devious and evil.

The hallway so dark behind him, I barely catch Andres getting into a prone position just beyond an open doorway.

"So, what do you want?" I begin to taunt Eduardo, needing to get him away from Isabella, "The keys to the warehouses? Me to write it on a piece of paper that I'm giving you my cartel?"

"You have always thought you were funny and charming," he lets go of Isabella and takes a step to the side so that he can walk around the chair.

Andres fires his rifle, placing a round through Eduardo's knee. The joint nearly explodes from the impact and drops him to his knees on the floor.

Throwing myself to ground, I dive for one of my guns. As I do, Andres puts a second bullet through Eduardo's shoulder, causing him to drop the gun in his hand.

Scrambling to my feet with the gun in my hand, I stalk toward Eduardo. Lifting my foot, I shove my boot into the fresh wound of his shoulder to push him to the ground.

"Think about fucking moving," I stare down at him, "And Andres is going to put another fucking bullet in you."

After pulling the knife from my pocket, I tear off my shirt and slide it over Isabella's head. I make quick work of cutting the zip ties from around Isabella's wrists and ankles, freeing her from the chair. After pulling the shirt over her naked body, I pull her into my arms and hold her close.

"I'm so fucking sorry, *cerecita*," she melts into me and sobs as I stroke her hair, "So sorry."

Her arms wrap around my neck, and she squeezes me tightly.

"Is there anyone else here?" I ask her as Andres crosses the room.

"No," she squeaks out between her tears.

"I need to put you down for a minute, okay?"

Isabella nods at me and loosens her grip around my neck so that I can place her on the ground.

It's fucking painful to let her go.

Andres stands over Eduardo with the muzzle of the rifle shoved in his face, as I dig through his pockets and check for other weapons. Finding a handful of zip ties, I grip the front of his shirt and lift him from the ground, "Get in the fucking chair."

thirty nine

ISABELLA

Watching Alex zip tie Eddie to the chair, I try to speak, but I can't get the words to come out.

"There's men coming," the words whisper over my lips so quietly that I barely hear them.

Both Alex and Andres have their attention on Eddie.

"You're going to fucking pay for even thinking you could lay a finger on her," Alex swings his fist at Eddie's face, "Slowly and painfully."

He hits him again and again, causing Eddie to spit blood onto his shirt.

"Alex," my words still inaudible, "Baby. There are men coming."

Walking from where Alex and Andres are beating Eddie, I cross the room to the gun still laying on the floor. Silently, I bend down and grab the cold metal with my hand.

"He has men coming for me," the words suddenly bellow from my mouth and fill the room.

Alex and Andres both turn toward my voice, as I lift the gun in their direction. They both step away from Eddie, assuming I'm going to shoot him.

Squeezing the trigger, I unload the magazine into the doorway at the back of the room. An older is clutching his gut, with a cigar still in his hand, as he staggers into the room.

Andres runs to the man, hitting him with the butt of his rifle as Alex runs to me.

"They were coming for me," I shake my head as he gently takes the gun from my hands, "Coming to take me. Eddie told me..."

"Shhhh," Alex pulls me tight and strokes my hair.

"He told me what they were going to do with me," I continue to shake in Alex's hold, "I can't. No one should."

"I know," he continues to comfort me, "I've got you. No one is taking you."

Cupping the sides of my head with both hands, he speaks against my lips, "No one will ever take you from me."

His hands slide over my ears just in time to muffle to more rifle shots. When he releases his hold, I turn to find that Andres has fired two rounds into the man laying at his feet.

"I'm going to check the hall," Andres yells across the room, "and get some things from the car."

"Did he hurt you?" Alex holds me against his chest, crooking his neck to look down at me.

From the pain in my face, I know it's obvious he hurt me. But I don't think that's what Alex means.

"Did he violate you?" He kisses my forehead, "Did he touch what is mine?"

"*Cerecita*," he strokes my hair, "I need to know. If he did, I intend to feed him his own cock before I kill him."

"No," I shake my head, "He didn't."

A look of both relief for me and disappointment about Eddie washes over Alex's face.

When Andres returns, he's carrying three plastic containers generally used for gasoline. Placing them on the ground, he grips the shirt of the dead man and drags him to Eddie's feet.

"Not to influence your plans for this piece of shit," Andres punches Eddie and gestures to the containers he was carrying, "I thought this was only fitting."

"Nostalgic even," Alex responds.

With his arm still wrapped around my shoulders, the three of us walk to the containers. Opening them, we begin splashing gasoline around the room.

Smelling the fumes, Eddie begins to yell and beg for his life. No one responds to him, and neither Alex nor Andres go near him. They both leave him for me.

Walking to the middle of the room, I pour gasoline over the dead man laying at Eddie's feet. Stepping behind him, I hear him grit, "Stupid fucking whore."

Lifting the near empty container, I empty the remaining contents over Eddie's head. He begins to gag and choke as the fumes likely burn his eyes and lungs.

"Call me what you want," I drop the container behind his chair, "This stupid fucking whore is about to send you to hell where you belong."

Walking away from him, I hear him begging for his life. When I reach the doorway Alex and Andres are standing in, Alex hands me the dead man's cigar. I hold it in my hand for a moment, contemplating what it is I am about to do. The line I am about to cross.

"You don't have to," Alex says as I flick the cigar into a puddle of gasoline, igniting a trail of fire around the room to a screaming Eddie.

By the time the three of us make our way outside, Eddie's screams have stopped. Standing in the middle of the overgrown parking lot, Alex wraps his arms around me from behind and pulls me back to his body.

With Andres standing beside us, we stand in silence as we watch the fire slowly overtake the building. I don't know exactly why this is so important to the two of them, but all of us wait until it is engulfed in flames before we're ready to leave.

forty

ALEJANDRO

With Isabella on my lap in the front seat, Andres drives us straight to the villa. Helping with the door to get her inside, he is about to leave.

"Stay," I turn to him, "Take the guest room, brother."

"Are you sure?" He questions.

"Yes," Isabella replies, "He's sure."

Andres awkwardly steps into the villa and Isabella turns to him, "Don't be weird about it. This isn't going to be some why choose romance book moment. We're offering you the guest room."

"Why choose?" Andres begins to question before he makes the connection.

When he does, Isabella wholeheartedly laughs.

I have missed that sound these past couple of days.

Isabella gives Andres a hearty hug before stretching up onto her toes to kiss his jaw, "Thank you."

Not knowing how to respond, he dips his head.

Holding Isabella's small hand in mine, I lead her down the hallway toward the master bedroom. Closing the door, I head to the bathroom and turn on the shower.

"Make sure it's hot," she calls from the doorway, and I smile back at her.

She pulls off my shirt and steps into the shower as I rest against the counter.

"Are you going to stand out there and gawk at me," she eyes me through the glass, "or are you going to come help me wash the blood out of my hair?"

Removing my boots and pants, I step into the shower with her, and she immediately wraps her arms around me. Holding her, I delicately wash her hair and carefully clean her bruised body.

As I do, she tells me everything she remembers about the time Eduardo held her captive. When I bend to wash her stomach, I notice the bruise running across it.

"He kicked me," she swallows hard as I stand to hug her tightly.

"It's early," I hold her against me under the spray of the water, "I'm sure everything is fine."

I feel her nod her head against my chest.

"I'll get the hospital to send over a doctor, just to be sure," I squeeze her tighter, "Okay?"

"Yes," she nods her head faster, "Please."

Stepping from the shower, I grab a towel and wrap it around my waist, leaving Isabella in the shower as I go to grab my phone.

Within the hour, the local hospital has a doctor at our villa with a portable ultrasound machine. Sitting on the bed next to Isabella, I hold her hand, both of us waiting impatiently for the doctor to get started.

He squeezes a cold gel onto her stomach and smears it around with the ultrasound probe. Moving it around, he looks at Isabella, "How far along are you?"

"About ten weeks?"

Continuing to move the probe around her stomach, he eventually stops and presses a button on the machine. The rapid sound of the baby's heartbeat fills the room.

"Everything looks perfectly fine," the doctor responds, before turning off the machine and wiping the gel from her stomach.

He looks her over a little more and let us know that the bruises and cuts on her face appear to be superficial. It doesn't look as though anything is broken and she should be pretty healed up physically in about a week, but mentally it might take a little longer.

Figuring there was no better place to recuperate than in paradise, I forced Isabella to stay in Mexico for the week.

Her face still has some remnants of the bruises from Eduardo, but he didn't manage to affect her smile at all. I've seen it plenty this week, most of all when I agreed to her request.

"Really?" She seems almost giddy, "Considering what happened to you there too, I didn't know if you would go for it."

"Absolutely, yes."

"I was lucky enough that you and Andres got to me in time, but that isn't the case for so many other women and children. I was reading and it affects almost five million women a year."

"I think it's an amazing idea, *cerecita*."

"A shelter for women and children affected by sex trafficking. Where they can heal. Where they can help each other."

"It will be incredible," I kiss her forehead, "You will make it incredible."

forty one

ISABELLA

EIGHTEEN MONTHS LATER

"Rafael," I speak firmly into the phone, "I don't care what the problem is. It needs to be taken care of by next week."

There are perks to your husband being the boss of the largest drug cartel in the world. Money. And power.

After I shared my idea with him, Alex wasted no time buying the Saint Francis property and the twenty acres around it. We have essentially built an entire city on the property, complete with medical and mental health facilities staffed entirely by female physicians. All ancillary staff we hired are women as well, quite a few of whom are survivors of sex trafficking rings around the world.

When word got out about what we were doing, so many people stepped forward to help in whatever way they were able. The support has been so overwhelming that after the opening next week, we are beginning construction on another facility in California with a few more to follow throughout the country within the year.

"Rafael," I repeat myself, "I don't care. Get it figured out. Get them to work overtime. I don't want a single man on that property when we open the doors next week. Figure. It. Out."

Hanging up the phone, I hear Alex walking onto the balcony behind me, "Fuck. My wife is a real boss bitch. That shit is hot."

"Alex," I stand from my chair to find him standing immediately behind me.

"I just put Jorge down for bed," he growls in my ear as his fingers immediately go for the button at the top of my pants.

"Let me just put my stuff away," my head melts into his shoulder as he slides his hand down the front of my pants.

"No. My son already cockblocked me this morning," I hear him chuckle before he wraps his fingers around my throat, "I'm not waiting another fucking minute."

His fingers rub over my clit for a moment before he pulls them from my pants. Roughly, his hands immediately yank them over my hips and down my legs. The moment he has them off me, he pulls my shirt over my head.

With his lips on my neck, he quickly works to remove his clothes as well. Leaving both of us naked under the stars on the balcony.

His lips trailing down my spine, he bends me over the concrete railing of the balcony. Kneeling behind me, his face is immediately between my thighs, with his tongue aggressively licking at my clit.

"I want to taste you coming all over my tongue," he growls against me before continuing to lap at me.

As I'm getting close, he groans with delight against me. The vibrations from him are my undoing, and I come undone as my hips continue to ride along his face.

"I'm never going to get enough of that," his lips press to my spine as he slowly slides himself inside of me.

His first thrust is hard and brutal, as he drives himself into me. Gripping me tightly, he savagely fucks me from behind. Pushing my hands against the wall, I straighten my arms and push back into his thrusts.

"Does my greedy little girl need more of my cock?" he growls as his hips work harder and faster against me.

"Yes," I scream out, "Please."

"You beg so nicely," he slams into me hard, "It's impossible to deny you what you want."

Another release crashes through my body, but Alex doesn't stop. He continues to drive into me hard and fast, his fingers now on my clit, causing me to come again and again.

"My good little girl, taking my cock, with our whole fucking empire able to watch me ravage their queen," he relentlessly continues to thrust into me, "all of them knowing I'd kill every last one of them that even dared to look at you."

"Fuck, Alex," I cry out as he brings me over the edge again, my whole body trembling against him.

"Coming for me again and again," he slows his thrusts, "taking my cock until I'm ready to fill you with my cum."

"Please," I beg, my body quickly becoming exhausted from the orgasms raging through me, yet still wanting more.

"Tell me," he growls as his fingers rake down my back, "Tell me what you want."

"I need...you...," I pant, barely able to say the words, "to fill me...until I'm dripping your cum."

"Such a dirty little girl," he grips my hips tightly and plows into me repeatedly, like a man determined to give his woman exactly what it is I am asking for. My legs tremble and I'm barely able to stand when he drives into me hard one final time.

"Fuck," he roars behind me, his hips quivering against my ass as he unloads his release inside of me.

Wrapping his arms around my hips, he grinds himself into me. Slow and deep as his lips pepper kisses along my shoulder and up my neck, "I fucking love you, *cerecita*."

you may choose to look the other way, but you can never again say that you did not know. ~william wilberforge

If you, or someone you know, may be a victim of human trafficking there are resources worldwide to help.

United States   888-373-7888
Canada   833-900-1010
United Kingdom   08000 121 700
Mexico   800-5533-000
India   +91-11-42244224
Australia   131 237
Germany   +49 157 537 309 86
Austria   +43 1-796 92 98
Bulgaria   +359 800 20 100
Denmark   +45 7020 2550
Finland   +358 29 54 63 177
Ireland   +353 1 9131528
Italy   800 290 290

thank you for reading

I hope you enjoyed Alejandro and Isabella's story!

If you did, the best support you can give to an indie author, like myself, is to tell others about my book. Reviews left on Goodreads, Amazon, or anywhere else you are comfortable truly mean the world to me.

Alejandro and Isabella's story is the first of a series. Want to know what happens next? Check out book two of the series, *Crave*.

www.ingramcontent.com/pod-product-compliance
Lightning Source LLC
Chambersburg PA
CBHW070505300726
48975CB00007B/2325